Time And Again

by

Nancy Fraser

Time And Again

Contact Information: info@thewildrosepress.com

The Wild Rose Press
PO Box 708
Adams Basin, NY 14410-0706
Visit us at www.thewildrosepress.com

Publishing History
First Faery Rose Edition, 2009
Second Faery Rose Edition 2016
Print ISBN: 1-60154-461-8

Published in the United States of America

Reaching out, Matt took hold of her elbow, pulling her up to the next crossbar until they shared one rung, their legs touching thigh to thigh. Turning her around so that she stood balanced in front of him, he pressed her hands flat against the small, metal square and fanned his own hands over hers.

She closed her eyes and let the overwhelming heat of Matt's body wash through her. *Nothing's changed. He can still jerk your heartstrings with little more than a touch.*

"Okay, Kate, on the count of three, we push. Got it?"

"Yes, I've got it."

"One," Matt began, "two, three."

At his mark, she pushed with all her might. Against her arms, his muscles bunched and strained. With a second effort, and then a third, they displaced the heavy lid and slid it to one side. Together, they stepped onto the next rung and poked their heads through the narrow opening.

"Holy Pulitzer Prize!"

"What the hell?" Matt said at the same time.

"What is all this, Matt?"

"I'm not sure, Cricket."

Like the beam of a maritime sentry, a wide and bright light swept over them, temporarily blinding them, instinctively forcing her backward and into Matt's arms. The beam swung to the left and then to the right, illuminating a vast room filled with blinking lights and computers. A small, circular drone buzzed around the room. The high tech set up resembled something straight out of *Star Wars*.

"Where are we?" Matt wondered aloud, his lips hovering close to her ear. The eerie uncertainty of his question sent a chill down her back.

"More importantly," she responded, her voice filled with a nervous excitement, "*when* are we?"

Praise for *Time and Again...*

"This book caught me from the first word and didn't let go until I finished it three hours later.

Fraser did an excellent job with world building, characterization and dialogue. I saw the future--both the good and the frightening aspects of it. I enjoyed how, despite advances in technology, people are still as flawed as always.

If you like witty romances with a paranormal/sci-fi/time-travel bent, you are going to love this one." - Reviewed by Water Lily ~ Long and Short Reviews.

Dedication

For Dawson, Mackenzie, Haley, Anya and William –
you will all live in a time that Grandma
can only write about. Enjoy!

PROLOGUE

Manhattan, Three Years Earlier

The sterile white walls of Lenox Hill hospital closed in on Matt; the antiseptic odor of the ICU filled his head, unsettling his stomach. Suspended somewhere between wishful thinking and reality, he watched through tear-clouded eyes while Kate fought tenaciously for her life. For the past thirty-six hours he'd stood at the foot of her bed, helpless to do anything but pray.

He blamed himself. If he'd been with Kate, if he'd kept their lunch date, she wouldn't be here now, tethered to enough damned machines to power the entire Upper East Side. He wouldn't be here, like this, praying for Kate's life and mourning all they'd already lost.

But no, not him. He'd called her at the last minute with an excuse: an extra shift...a chance to possibly catch the bad guys in the act. For the sake of making the city a little safer, he'd nearly sacrificed the one person he loved most. When he'd called, he'd expected her to rant and rave, to remind him of all the other lunches they'd missed, of the burnt roasts and canceled plans. Yet, she hadn't. She'd not argued at all. She'd just accepted.

Matt closed his eyes and silently recited the promises he'd made over and over again in the last day and a half; asked for the umpteenth time for the chance to make things better between him and Kate. For a chance—

"Hey, bro, how you holding up?"

The sound of Jim's voice wrapped around Matt like a welcome security blanket.

1

"Just like Kate, I'm hanging on." His gaze fell to the chart in his brother's hands. "You've got the lab reports?"

"Not yet. They should be coming up any minute."

"What can you tell me *now*?"

"Not much, other than what we already know. No sign of outward trauma. No indication of prior illness." Methodically, Jim tapped his finger against her chart, emphasizing each point. "For all intents and purposes," he continued, "Kate's as healthy as a horse."

"Then why is she lying there just two breaths short of death?"

Jim laid a hand on Matt's shoulder and squeezed, offering without words his love and strength. "She's making progress and her condition's been upgraded from critical to serious. You know Kate, she's not—"

"Excuse me, Dr. Kelly," the nurse interrupted. "I've got the lab results."

"Thanks," he said, taking the papers from the nurse's hand.

"Well?" Matt demanded, barely giving him time to scan the results.

With a dismissive wave of his hand and a faint lifting of his eyebrows, Jim flipped over the first page and went on to the second. Rushing him, Matt realized, would be futile. Thorough to the bone, Jim analyzed everything to the extreme.

"Well?" He repeated, silently hating the very traits that made Jim an excellent physician.

In a habitual gesture, Jim removed his glasses and tucked them into the breast pocket of his lab coat. "According to the blood tests, Kate has ingested a large quantity of a drug similar to UG-32."

"UG-32?"

"It's a drug given to rape victims within the first

twenty-four hours to abort a possible pregnancy."

"That can't be," Matt denied. "You said 'similar to', but not exactly, right? I mean, it could be some other drug."

"It has all the properties of UG-32, plus some additional chemical makeup with which I'm unfamiliar. The secondary compounds in this drug don't exist, at least not to the collective knowledge of anyone here at Lenox Hill."

"So, what you're saying is, there's a crackpot out there somewhere making designer drugs with untried chemicals."

Jim nodded, and Matt asked, "But why? If this UG-32 does the same thing, why would there be a need for a black market substitute?"

"Availability most likely. UG-32 is a controlled substance and requires a prescription."

"How'd Kate get it?"

"You sound as if you think she took it on purpose."

Matt shook his head. Vehemently, he said, "No, not Kate. Someone gave it to her. They slipped it into her food or, maybe, into her water."

"But who?" Jim asked. "Who's she ticked off lately—other than you, that is?"

"Knowing Kate, it must have been someone important. Damnedest thing is, she promised to slow down. Maybe even quit entirely within the next month. Now, it's too late."

"Kate'll never quit," Jim told him. "She's too competitive. Without a story to chase, Kate wouldn't be the same woman you fell in love with and married."

Matt sighed deeply and pinched the bridge of his nose between his thumb and forefinger in an effort to dispel his headache. "Do me a favor, Jimbo, and keep an eye on her. I'll be back in an hour or so."

"No problem, bro. Where are you going?" Before

he could answer, Jim added, "Hopefully home to get some much needed rest."

"Down to the station. Something's not right here. I can feel it. Smell it. I want names and dates. I've been standing here for the past two days making myself a mental list of Kate's last few investigations and of anyone who'd have a reason to do this."

"And, what've you come up with?"

"Nothing, unfortunately. That's why I want to check in with the department."

"Stay calm, Matt," Jim reminded him. "This one's personal."

"You're damned right it is. Someone out there drugged my wife." Pausing only a moment, he added bitterly, "and murdered our baby."

ONE

Greenwich Village, Current Day
"Welcome to Madame Olga's. I am Lillie, Madame's assistant. Please come in and join the others."

Reluctantly, Kate followed the woman's lead, stepping across the threshold and into a foyer decorated in plush gold and deep purple. The pungent aroma of spicy incense assaulted her senses. Rather than soothe, as most incense did, this particular aroma seemed to heighten her awareness to a near-fever pitch, sending her pulse into overdrive, increasing her wariness from the very beginning.

"Right this way," Lillie told her. "The other guests are waiting."

"Thank you," she said, following closely in Lillie's wake, moving instinctively to the rhythm set by the ringing bells fastened to the woman's wrists and ankles.

The flowing skirts are a nice touch. Not to mention the gold hoop earrings and heavy makeup. A scene from a 60s B movie, complete with costumes. What's Cal Peters gotten me into this time?

Despite her intention to remain unaffected, she couldn't help but feel a bit apprehensive. There'd been so many surreal stories, so many unexplained phenomenon.

At the parlor door, Kate handed Lillie her jacket, then drew a deep breath and stepped inside. She'd never been to a séance before. Nor had she ever had her palm read, or her cards done. It all seemed so hokey.

Four other guests stood around a large circular table. Positioned in the very center of the room and covered with a dark velvet cloth, it drew Kate's gaze. A crystal ball and deck of tarot cards sat in the middle of the table.

All the theatrical trappings of a supposed medium...

From her post at the door, Lillie told them, "Madame will join you shortly."

No sooner had she spoken when the lights flickered and a discretely concealed door on the opposite wall slid open. A matronly woman, dressed in flowing emerald-green robes, swept into the room so smoothly she could have been floating on a cloud.

How dramatic. What next? Will the table rise? Will the heavy brocade drapes billow even in the absence of a breeze? What does Madame Olga have in store for tonight's prey?

"Good evening, ladies and gentlemen," the woman said, "*I* am Madame Olga."

Kate gave the woman full points. Madame Olga possessed a very commanding presence. So much so, she barely noticed when the parlor door opened to admit one last guest.

"Ah," Madame crooned smoothly, "a late arrival. Welcome to Madame Olga's."

Kate looked toward the door. Her gaze settled on the tall man and met his own. His flared in recognition. She sucked in a deep breath. Her eyes widened in surprise.

Matthew.

What is he doing here? More importantly, what could the N.Y.P.D. possibly want with a small time operator like Olga Limas? Suddenly, the fluff piece of journalism Kate had been anticipating became something far more interesting and infinitely more newsworthy.

"Please," Madame Olga invited, "let us all be seated."

It would have been too much, Kate supposed, to expect that he might have chosen a seat on the opposite side of the table. No, not Matt. *He* had to take the chair directly to her left.

Leaning close, he whispered, "What the hell are you doing here, Kate?"

"None of your business, Matt," she whispered back.

"Are you on an assignment?"

"*None of your business*," she repeated, more stridently this time.

Matt rolled his eyes in an exaggerated show of impatience. Very sharply, he told her, "Dammit Kate, you're in the wrong place at the wrong time. *As usual.*"

"I'm not—" she began, her well-honed rebuttal interrupted by a swell of music and the metallic clink of Madame Olga's gold bangle bracelets.

"Tonight," Madame Olga began, "we will attempt to venture beyond reality. We will try, through the power of our minds, to communicate with the other side. With any luck, one of you will be chosen for the experience of a lifetime."

"What experience is that, Madame Olga?" Matt asked.

Silently, Kate fumed. That should have been her question.

"Why, traveling to the future, of course. Isn't that why some of you are here?"

Hushed whispers circulated from person to person. While the others seemed in awe of the adventure the medium promised, Kate sensed Matt's disbelief as strongly as her own. Perhaps, together, they'd be able to uncover Madame Olga's secrets.

Together. The thought conjured up unwanted, yet unstoppable, memories.

Madame Olga took the hand of the man at her right and held it in hers. "What is your name?" she asked.

"Joe. Joe Waldman."

Stroking his weathered hand with her bejeweled fingers, she said, "Madame Olga senses unease within you, Joseph Waldman. You miss your late wife and wish to know that she is at peace."

"Yes," the man said solemnly. His voice filled with emotion, his eyes with tears.

Madame Olga spoke to each person in turn, taking their hand in hers, using her *powers* to divine their needs. As she had with Joe Waldman, she correctly identified each of the next three guests' reasons for seeking audience with a spiritualist.

When Kate's turn came, she reluctantly put her hand in Madame Olga's. The mere touch of the medium's fingertips sent a shock through her hand and arm. Madame Olga obviously felt it as well, for she quickly released Kate's hand only to take it up again a moment later.

"What is your name?" Madame Olga asked.

"Kate...Kate Brogan."

"Well, Kate Brogan, Madame Olga senses a power within you. An electricity. You are curious by nature, and—"

"Amen," Matt muttered at Kate's side.

"Shh," Kate admonished, fixing him with what she hoped to be a quelling glare.

"Madame Olga also senses a deeply buried hostility between you and the gentlemen at your side. You were once lovers, perhaps?"

"Something like that," Matt said sharply.

"And you," Madame asked, "what is your name?"

"Matthew Kelly."

"Detective Kelly, I would believe," Madame Olga said. "You are a police detective, are you not?"

"Yes," Matt admitted.

A second murmur worked its way through the room, dying down when Matt asked, "Should I leave, Madame Olga?"

"No, Detective Kelly, Madame Olga welcomes your scrutiny. I have nothing to hide and everything to prove. All I ask is that, when you see the power Madame Olga possesses for yourself, you will let me be and allow me to earn an *honest* living."

"Fair enough," Matt agreed.

"Good. Now, let us join hands."

With the circle of hands complete, Madame Olga closed her eyes. Her head fell forward. The lights dimmed and then went out completely, leaving them bathed in nothing more than the glow of a handful of candles spread randomly around the room. The music, barely audible before, swelled slowly and then fell silent.

Kate sat as still as a statue, holding her breath, waiting, for what she wasn't sure. Madame Olga held tightly to her right hand. Matt held even tighter to her left. Kate wanted to pull free of Matt's hold, to escape the memory-inducing warmth of his grasp. Yet, to do so would break the psychic bond Madame Olga had set out to establish.

Listen to yourself, Brogan. You sound like a convert. A believer. Peters'll have your butt on a platter if you mess this up. You're here to do a job, nothing more. And certainly nothing less.

Madame Olga chanted, her voice changing from high-pitched squeal to deep growl, and back again. Her words changed from English, to very rudimentary Spanish, to some strange dialect Kate had never heard.

The candles flickered, sending shadows dancing across the room. Madame Olga's chanting stopped. The inflection of her voice changed. "Joseph," she said, "are you there?"

"Helga, darling," Joe Waldman answered, "Is

that you?"

Kate felt herself being tugged in Matt's direction. Automatically, and most infuriatingly, she leaned closer. Next to her ear, he whispered, "Oh, brother, how corny can you get?"

"Shh." Despite her admonishment, she couldn't deny having the same thought herself.

"I am happy, Joseph. I am at peace."

Madame Olga slumped forward, her head nearly touching the smooth velvet cloth.

"Is there more?" Joe Waldman asked.

"She is gone," Madame said simply. "I feel another presence waiting. I need a moment."

The chanting began again and, as before, Madame Olga's voice changed. Her tone deep and guttural, her accent Bronx-thick, she called out a name. "Gloria. Gloria, baby."

"Harvey?" The blonde sitting directly opposite Kate responded eagerly. "Is that you, Harvey?"

"Yeah," came the reply. "Whatta 'ya want, baby?"

Kate watched the woman named Gloria with interest, wondering if she worked for the medium as a plant.

The woman swallowed hard, visibly shaken by having made contact with what she obviously believed to be the *other side*. Her frightened vulnerability was as vivid as the bright red lipstick and thick, fake eyelashes she wore. Gloria seemed genuine.

"I want," she began, then swallowed again. "I want to know what you did with my diamond necklace!"

Kate couldn't help the chuckle that escaped her throat. Nor could she halt the quickening of her pulse when Matt squeezed her hand in acknowledgment of the infinitesimal slip.

Madame Olga slumped forward again, but not

before saying one final word in *Harvey's* deep voice, "Wife."

"You gave it to your wife? Why you sleazy son-of-a—"

Gloria, Kate imagined, would have gladly continued her diatribe had Madame Olga not sat up suddenly, her breathing ragged and her head bobbing around like a plastic dog in the back window of some teenager's souped-up car.

"The guide," Madame said dramatically. "I feel his presence. He has come to escort one of you to the future. Everyone. Quickly. Close your eyes. *Feel* his strength."

Kate had no intention of closing her eyes. Whatever happened next would be etched in her memory forever. This entire hokey routine would soon be uncovered. Yet, when Madame spoke next, Kate's eyes closed of their own accord.

"Come to us, oh learned one," Madame cajoled, "show us the way to the future. Show us your power."

Kate tried time and again to open her eyes. Unexplainably, she felt lightheaded. Dizzy. She *had* to keep her wits about her. She couldn't let Madame Olga fool her. She couldn't...

Suddenly, and without warning, Kate began floating upward. How could she have missed the wires on her chair?

Face it, Brogan, you blew it. Seeing Matt again is playing havoc with your head, and ruining your reporter's sixth-sense.

"The guide has arrived," Madame announced. "He has chosen. Whomever he takes, remember to let go of your neighbor's hand. Do not be afraid. You will not be harmed."

A second wave of dizziness washed over her. The table moved. Or, did she? The others were drifting farther and farther away. Madame Olga released

Kate's hand.

"It is Kate the guide has chosen," Madame Olga told them. "Relax, Kate Brogan. Relax and accept that you are the one."

Kate wiggled her fingers, doing her best to dispel the tingle invading her entire body. Her left hand remained captive in Matt's tight grip.

"*Let go*," she said insistently, tugging on her hand for emphasis. "You heard Madame Olga, I'll be fine."

"I'm not letting go, Kate," he said stubbornly.

"But, you must!" Madame Olga warned. "The guide chooses only one."

A blinding flash of light shone from overhead, penetrating her closed eyelids. Someone screamed and Kate heard her own voice echoing around her. She felt herself being pulled, lifted, and then thrown. From deep within, she heard herself calling Matt's name. Yet, when she opened her mouth to speak, no audible sound emerged.

An eerie stillness and quiet engulfed her.

She felt cold. Frigid.

Gradually, her head stopped spinning and Kate opened her eyes. The candles were snuffed out, replaced by a subdued light of undetermined origin. Everything looked different. There were no chairs. No table. She couldn't see Madame Olga or the others. Not even Matt. A sudden sense of foreboding came over her when she realized Matt no longer held her hand.

Her stomach roiled, much like the first time she and Matt had gone sailing. Much like those first early mornings...and then that horrible night in the hospital when...

She drew a deep, steadying breath, wishing both the queasiness and the memories away.

"Kate," Madame Olga called out. "Where are you, Kate?"

"Here," she said.

"Kate, answer Madame Olga."

"*I am. Can't you hear me?*"

Rather than an affirmative response to her shouted demand, she heard Madame Olga ask, "Where's the other one? The detective?"

"He's gone, too," someone said.

"That can't be," Madame Olga denied. "The guide can take only one. The void between here and there is very fragile. Two bodies might displace the entire transportation."

"What'll happen now?" Another guest asked.

"I don't know," Madame admitted. "I truly don't know."

Kate strained to hear more but the voices were fading quickly.

"Where am I?" Kate demanded loudly, mentally willing that Madame Olga hear her.

"You mean, where are *we*?" The sound of Matt's deep baritone spun her around. Seeing him there, although barely visible in the hazy gray light, somehow reassured her. Comforted her.

"Matt?"

"Yeah, Cricket, I'm right here."

Despite her fear of this strange place, she couldn't help but react to the nickname she'd once loved and now hated in equal measure. The nickname she'd not heard in two long, lonely years.

"Don't call me that," she told him angrily. Defensively.

"Sorry, Kate. Old habits and all."

"Where are we?" she asked.

"We've obviously been lifted by some sort of guide wires through a hole in the ceiling. Most likely, we're somewhere in the dear Madame's attic."

"It's awfully cold in here," Kate pointed out rather needlessly, rubbing her hands up and down her arms in a vain search for warmth.

"Do you want my jacket?" Matt asked.

"No, I'll be okay. Let's just get out of here."

"Sure thing, Cri...ah...Kate. Right away."

Kate took two steps in Matt's direction. Beneath her feet, the floor felt like marshmallows.

"What is this stuff?" she asked.

"Some sort of soft foam base, I'd guess." Easing them cautiously forward, he grudgingly admitted, "I'll give the old broad this, she knows her special effects. What little we can see in this limited light looks real enough. Next thing you know she'll have little green men coming out of the closets."

"Spare me. Please. All I want right now is to get into my car and go home."

"You never did tell me why you were here in the first place," he reminded her.

"It's none—"

"So help me, Kate, if you say *none of my business*, I'll leave you here and go off and find my own way out. Until then, we're not moving an inch unless you talk."

Defiantly, she put her hands on her hips and glared at him, hating his patience and wishing she hadn't tested it once too often. Finally, she admitted, "Cal Peters sent me to do a follow-up story. Over the past few months we've been watching Madame Olga's operation."

"Somehow, I can't imagine Peters wasting his best reporter on a small time operator like Olga Limas."

Best reporter. Kate wanted to revel in Matt's compliment. Yet, to do so, would be the same as admitting she still cared about his opinion. Instead, she told him, "The assignment surprised me, too. We got a tip that something big was supposed to happen at tonight's séance. Whoever the caller was, he suggested Cal might want to send me."

"What's your research got you so far on Olga

Limas?" Matt asked.

"Nothing concrete. One of our reporters, Kevin Johnson, came to Madame Olga's with a group from his lodge. Now, mind you, Kevin's a middle-aged man and definitely not prone to exaggeration. Yet, when he told Cal about talking to his dead father, he truly believed it had happened. Then, last month on a follow-up visit, Josh Taylor watched one of his fellow attendees disappear into thin air only to return moments later."

"Hank Belcher?"

"Yeah, how'd you know?"

"His name came up in our investigation. What'd Belcher tell your reporter?"

"He claimed to have been transported into the future. He told Josh he'd seen strange-looking buildings and rooms made of glass with no visible doors. He said the people were not much different than today, except everyone looked young. Almost ageless. They spoke very little but what they said sounded stilted. Formal. Unfortunately, the more Josh questioned him, the less Belcher remembered. By the end of the interview, he'd become disoriented and forgotten everything. When Josh called him on it, he denied everything. How about you? What's vice got on Madame Olga?"

He paused for a moment, as if reluctant to share his information. Or, possibly, she suspected, he wanted to pick and choose the right words. *Come on Matt, say something. We're not married any more. You can talk to me now.*

Just when she thought he meant not to answer at all, he said, "It seems Olga Limas, a.k.a. Madame Olga, did a private séance for a city councilman's wife. According to a couple of eye-witnesses, Madame Olga allegedly dredged up the woman's dead first husband. The lady hasn't been the same since. The councilman's asked for a full investigation."

"Let's get out of here," she said suddenly, the goose-bumps on her arms a by-product of more than just the cool, damp air.

Matt withdrew a pocket-sized flashlight from his jacket and switched it on. Then, taking hold of her hand, he started forward.

It didn't matter in which direction they went, they came upon a dead end: a wall with no door. When they'd back-tracked for the umpteenth time with no visible results, Matt drew to a halt.

"Why are we stopping?"

"I'm sure we've been this way before."

"No, we haven't," she insisted.

"Yes, we have," he argued back. "I'll prove it." Reaching into his pocket a second time, he withdrew an ink pen and double-clicked the point into place. "I'll just mark this wall..." he began, only to finish with, "Dammit, I broke my pen."

"How'd you manage that?"

"It's this wall," he told her. "It looks porous, kind of like cushioned paneling. Yet, the damned stuff's as dense as steel."

Matt ran his flattened palm over the wall a second time, and she watched the glide of his hand with an unwarranted amount of interest. Beneath the silk sleeve of her blouse, her skin quivered with a sudden tingle...an awareness...a memory.

"So much for that idea," he conceded.

"How about lipstick?" Kate asked, reaching into her purse and withdrawing a shiny gold tube. "Would that work?"

Purely by instinct, she imagined, Matt reached out and squeezed her shoulder. "Great idea, sweetheart! That's my—"

His words fell away as quickly as his hand, leaving her teetering on the edge of some great emotional abyss—bereft of both his praise and his touch.

Again they started out, Matt holding the flashlight and Kate coating the wall, from time to time, with peach-toned lipstick. For over an hour, they went forward, and back, and forward. They turned left and then right, only to come across another of her markings.

"Whoever said X marks the spot," she joked nervously, "didn't know the half of it."

"We can stop," Matt suggested, adding, "that is, if you're getting tired."

"The only thing I'm tired of is this maze and Madame Olga's trickery. I want out, and I want out now."

Now seemed to be taking forever. They'd wandered in circles for what seemed like an eternity, when they finally stumbled on a new and unfamiliar passageway. Cautiously, they ventured forward.

"Matt, look!"

"I see it, Kate." Matt reached out and grasped the strange-looking apparatus in front of them, adding, "I'm just not sure what it is?"

Kate brushed past him. Grabbing onto the same bar he still held, she shook it soundly. "It's a ladder. Anyone can see that."

"It's not like any ladder I've ever seen."

She studied the mass of steel beams and cross bars intently. The rather crude contraption resembled something constructed from a child's erector set. Crisscrossing upward, the girders went at least two hundred feet in the air or more. Straight up.

"I'm going to try climbing up these beams," Matt told her. "You wait here."

"No way, Matt. You're not leaving me behind."

He paused, as if he wanted to argue the point. Yet when he started forward she followed closely behind and he did nothing to stop her.

Slowly, they climbed one section of beams at a time. With each step they took, each rung they climbed, her trepidation grew. A million questions buzzed through her head.

What's happening here? Why are we climbing this thing? Exactly, where are we?

"Matt?" she called out.

"Yeah, Cricket."

Kate let the slip pass in favor of asking, "What if we really did get transported somewhere? Other than Madame Olga's attic, I mean."

"That's not possible."

"Then how do you explain a maze larger than your average attic, and climbing this...this ladder? We're getting nowhere fast."

Matt sighed deeply, and then stopped a moment to press his thumb and forefinger to the bridge of his nose.

An old habit. She steeled herself against the memories conjured up by even the simplest of Matt's gestures. Luckily, she didn't have time to dwell on the past before they were moving again. Onward and upward...higher and higher. Just when she thought they'd never reach the top, Matt stopped.

"We've made it, Kate!"

"Made it where?"

"To the top of whatever. There's a trap door."

"Can you open it?"

"I think so."

Matt flattened his hands against the metal door and pushed. Nothing happened. "This isn't as easy as it looks. Maybe you'd better lend a hand."

Reaching out, Matt took hold of her elbow, pulling her up to the next crossbar until they shared one rung, their legs touching thigh to thigh. Turning her around so that she stood balanced in front of him, he pressed her hands flat against the small, metal square and fanned his own hands over hers.

She closed her eyes and let the overwhelming heat of Matt's body wash through her. *Nothing's changed. He can still jerk your heartstrings with little more than a touch.*

"Okay, Kate, on the count of three, we push. Got it?"

"Yes, I've got it."

"One," Matt began, "two, three."

At his mark, she pushed with all her might. Against her arms, his muscles bunched and strained. With a second effort, and then a third, they displaced the heavy lid and slid it to one side. Together, they stepped onto the next rung and poked their heads through the narrow opening.

"Holy Pulitzer Prize!"

"What the hell?" Matt said at the same time.

"What is all this, Matt?"

"I'm not sure, Cricket."

Like the beam of a maritime sentry, a wide and bright light swept over them, temporarily blinding them, instinctively forcing her backward and into Matt's arms. The beam swung to the left and then to the right, illuminating a vast room filled with blinking lights and computers. A small, circular drone buzzed around the room. The high tech set up resembled something straight out of *Star Wars*.

"Where are we?" Matt wondered aloud, his lips hovering close to her ear. The eerie uncertainty of his question sent a chill down her back.

"More importantly," she responded, her voice filled with a nervous excitement, "*when* are we?"

TWO

"Look at them, Ezekiel. I thought you said early twenty-first century beings were inept and lacked initiative. You predicted it would take at least four hours for them to negotiate the maze and another hour and a half to climb the ladder. Instead, it has taken them only two and a half to do both. They are not exactly the lab rats you likened them to, are they?"

"What can I say? They were unexpectedly persistent."

"And, now, what will you do with them?"

"I am not sure. This was not supposed to happen. There should have only been one. *Only the woman.* Still, this should not stop us from accomplishing our initial objective."

"There will be no objective if the elders get wind of this. Your well-thought-out alteration has suddenly become complicated and dangerous, both to us and to history. Those who back us may not be as agreeable when they find out about the error."

"I will explain."

"Explain what, Ezekiel? What will you say? *Excuse me, gentlemen, but it seems there is a slight problem with our plan.* Do you think pleading human error will get you out of this?"

"Esther, please."

Shaking her head, Esther reached out and shut down the surveillance camera. "Come on," she told him. "We have guests to welcome."

****

"Like I said," Kate repeated, her deep sigh

warming Matt's soul like a shot of fifty-dollar scotch. "When and where are we?"

"Hell if I know, Cricket." Before she could demand a retraction of the nickname, he pressed two fingers to her perfectly kissable lips. "Sorry."

He waited for her rebuttal. Yet, it never came. Her usual bravado had wilted, replaced by an uncharacteristic nervousness. She looked endearingly innocent, frightened and, had he not known better, on the verge of tears. He dismissed that possibility immediately. Kate Brogan didn't cry.

Ever.

Not even when she should have...

She hadn't cried at their wedding; she surely hadn't cried at their divorce. She hadn't even cried when they'd lost the baby.

"So, what do we do now?" she asked.

"I guess we start poking around. There's got to be a way out of here somewhere."

They slid the trap door back in place, then walked the perimeter of the large room. Against three of the four walls were banks of computers, their shiny silver surfaces lit with a myriad of bright lights. Filled with numbers, the monitors blinked and whirled, changing constantly.

A solid glass window made up the fourth wall. Beyond the glass stood a cloudless, starless curtain of black.

"Let's go this way first," he suggested.

Kate, he quickly realized, wanted to go in the opposite direction.

Of course.

"That's just a window, Matt. I think we need to find some way out of this room."

"How about we split up? I'll check out the giant picture window and you look for a door.

She nodded. Yet, when he stepped forward, she held tightly to his hand. He tugged once, twice.

"On second thought," she conceded, "it might not be safe to split up."

"Good thinking, Kate. Let's go this way first." She hesitated for barely a heartbeat. Reluctant, he suspected, to give in so easily. He tugged on her hand one more time and finally she followed.

At the window, he pressed his nose to the glass, cupping his hands at his temples, blocking out all background light. Still, he could barely make out what lay beyond.

"Well?"

"See for yourself, Kate. There's nothing to see."

"Well then, why would I look?"

He chuckled. He couldn't help it, even though he knew Kate would take immediate offense.

"What's so funny?"

"Nothing, Kate. Look for yourself. It's pitch black out there."

Kate did as he had, pressing her nose to the glass and blocking out the light with her cupped hands.

"Anything?" he asked.

"No. Nothing at all."

About to suggest they move on, he stopped short when the lights dimmed, the computers shut down and the room behind them went completely dark

"Perhaps," a strange, sultry voice said, "this will help."

They turned in the direction of the woman's voice, yet there was no one there.

"Where are you?" he asked.

"Who are you?" Kate asked, almost in unison.

Not surprisingly, there was no response.

Matt turned back to the window, his gaze searching the horizon for something he could identify. What he found nearly stilled his wildly beating heart.

"Kate, look!"

"What?"

Laying his hands on her shoulders, he turned her toward the window and lifted her chin with his fingertips until her line of sight matched his own.

"Oh," she said, her voice catching. "Oh, my. Is that what I think it is?"

"Yeah, Cricket, it would seem so."

Kate shook her head. "It can't be. It's..." When the words wouldn't come, he drew her close and buried her face against his shoulder. Over the top of her head, he studied the landscape, his gaze coming back time and again to the pile of rubble off in the distance.

A maze of jagged edges, a half mask of a woman's serene smile, the rounded curve of a sculpted flame, the twisted remains of a spiral staircase, and the nearly indistinguishable heap of steel girders were all that was left of the Statue of Liberty.

Like something out of a vintage sci-fi movie, the damage appeared rampant, enormous. Complete. Devastating...

His arms tightened reflexively until Kate squirmed restlessly at his side. She stood there only moments longer before her innate instinct for survival took over, along with a stubborn curiosity like that which had plagued their marriage from the very start.

Laying her hands flat against his chest, she pushed.

Hard.

Anger tinting her cheeks a bright red, she stared out the window once more. Her hands balled into tight fists, and she pounded them against the glass.

"Darn it, Matt. How could this have happened? And...when? I mean...didn't we just finish repairing her."

"I'm not sure what happened, Kate. Or when."

"Any type of data retrieval you might require can be found in the computer banks to your left." The matter of fact tone of a man's voice made them both jump.

As quickly as they'd dimmed, the lights came up again and, when they turned around, they came face to face with a tall, bearded black man. In his hand, he held a device resembling a remote control. He didn't appear dangerous. If anything, his expression and demeanor were devoid of emotion of any type.

"Mr. and Mrs. Kelly, welcome to Analog Station Three. I must admit, we were not expecting two visitors. Having arrived together, you have breached all the known statistical norms of time teleportation."

"We have?" Kate asked. Almost as an afterthought, and much to Matt's consternation, she added, "We're not married anymore."

"Maybe not where you come from but, here, divorce is not recognized."

Matt shifted from one foot to the other, squaring his stance. "Where, *exactly*, is here? And, who are you?"

Before the stranger could answer, Kate added, "More importantly, *when* are we?

"I am Ezekiel Washington, your interzonal escort while you are here."

Kate pressed her hand against the window behind them, her voice soft, unsure. "Here, where?"

"New York City, of course. Not far from where you were when you left Madame Olga's parlor." Nodding toward the window, Ezekiel added, "I believe you have already seen one of our major tourist attractions."

Inwardly, Matt seethed. "Humor me, *Zeke*," he said testily, "what day, and year, is this?"

"December 16, 2065."

Matt put his arm around Kate's shoulders,

drawing her back to his side, certain their shared nightmare would end soon and that they'd be at home ensconced in their huge bed.

What bed, smart ass? She got the bed as part of the divorce settlement...along with your heart, and your soul.

His self-deprecating introspection came to an abrupt halt when Ezekiel said, "Follow me, Matthew and Kate. I will take you to the communal facilities."

"When do we go home?" Kate asked.

"So soon?" Ezekiel asked. "Most people would give one of their appendages for an opportunity like this. Why are you so eager to leave?"

"No reason, I guess. I'm just not sure I believe all this."

"And," Matt added, his grin solely for Kate and intended to tease, "She's hoping to make the wire service deadline. Imagine the scoop."

Kate glared at him, her bright emerald eyes shooting daggers, while her mouth trembled in an effort to keep from laughing; as always, a delightful contradiction.

"Well, Kate, I am truly distressed to disappoint you," their host said, "but you will not be leaving today. This scoop, whatever that is, will have to wait."

"You don't know what a scoop is?" Kate asked incredulously. "Everyone who's ever read a newspaper or an online news report knows what a scoop is. Where would Citizen Kane have been without a scoop, even a fictitious one? What about Clark Kent and Lois Lane? Why, everyone—"

"Newspapers, even most online versions, Kate," Ezekiel explained, "have been obsolete for nearly thirty years."

"Obsolete?" she repeated. "No newspapers?"

Chuckling, Matt admitted, "There's some good news amid the confusion. Too bad it didn't happen earlier, when I could have truly appreciated it."

Kate swatted his arm in mock anger, her touch reverberating through him clear down to the soles of his feet. Being this close to her had stirred up some pleasant, and not-so-pleasant, memories. Rather than let the long-buried emotions overwhelm him, he turned his thoughts back to the present—or was it the future—and asked, "Why can't we go home today? And, come to think of it, how do you know our names?"

"Like I said, you two are an unusual transportation. Ever since Madame Olga's psychic abilities began intruding on our peaceful little community, we have done our best to accommodate her unusual mental prowess. Everything had gone smoothly, up until now. Before I can risk sending you back, I will have to study my charts and consult the database. I would not want to send you back to the wrong time and place. As for knowing your names, we know everything about you, Matthew and Kate Kelley. We are an advanced society. Our methods of identification are advanced as well. The moment you and Kate stepped through the gateway, we knew who you were."

Ezekiel pointed the remote device toward what appeared to be a solid wall and pressed one of the two dozen or so buttons. A door slid upward, revealing a long corridor with smooth, tubular, aluminum-colored walls.

"Come along, Kate and Matthew. As long as you are here, you might as well experience some of our advanced culture."

****

Kate did her best to absorb everything she saw; everything she heard. Yet, other than the hum-drum activities of daily life, they'd been shown nothing out of the ordinary. She wanted more; she wanted to explore, examine, and record. She wanted to know which computers controlled what, what function each gadget performed, and when and how they'd be transported home.

All around her, computers hummed, yet nowhere did there appear to be any sort of data printout. Then there was the clothing. Strange, monk-like robes seemed to be the normal mode of dress.

People came and went, often stopping but not speaking, leaving Kate with the feeling that she and Matt were on display.

There's just too much to take in, and it's all so weird.

Matt, it seemed, had found other interests, other ways to soak up atmosphere—the two-legged, blonde brand of atmosphere.

It doesn't matter. After all, he is a free man.

"Esther said this is where they congregate," Matt told her. "They don't have organized religion like we're accustomed to but rather each person communes with their inner self."

"And just what communing did you and Esther do?"

Silently, she admonished herself for showing the least bit of interest. *I sound like a jealous shrew. If he laughs at me, I'll slap that grin right off his handsome face.* Beneath her breath, Kate swore.

"Actually, Esther and good-old Zeke do the communing around here. She's his wife. Life partner, I believe she called it."

"Really? But, he's so much older."

"Not really," Matt explained. "It seems the men age, but only to the point of becoming mature. The women never age past twenty-five, or so."

Kate snickered, and then tried to hide the sound behind a yawn.

"What's so funny, Cricket?"

Just so he wouldn't think she'd missed his slip of

the tongue, she glared at him, but then admitted, "I guess that, in this world, I'm an old lady at thirty-two."

"You don't look thirty-two. As a matter of fact, you don't look a day older than the day we—"

"Listen, Matt," she interrupted, cutting through his recollection, "we've got to find a way to take some of this back with us. I'll need proof, if I'm going to get that Pulitzer."

Nodding, he admitted, "You might as well go for the gold, Kate. After this little excursion, the N.Y.P.D.'s case against Madame Olga is shot to hell and back."

"What do you think they'll show us? How much will we be able to prove once we're home?"

"I don't know. Whatever it is, though, I have no doubt you'll make them believe you."

A door to the left slid open, revealing yet another long, sleek and totally innocuous corridor.

"It is supplement time," Esther announced. "Come, our evening meal awaits us."

Thankfully, food hadn't changed too much in nearly fifty years. Meat still tasted like meat, although Kate doubted she had the nerve to question the steak's origin. Just in case. Potatoes, although similar to those of the early twenty-first century, were less starchy, their texture surprisingly light and fluffy. The vegetables looked like something from the root family, their color anything but common.

"What is the matter, Kate?" Ezekiel asked. "Steamed beta root does not excite you?"

"It tastes fine," she explained, "it's the color I'm not quite used to."

"Kate has a thing about red," Matt pointed out. "It's not one of her favorite colors."

"Why not?" Esther questioned.

Matt grinned, and explained, "It clashes with

her hair."

She wanted to reach out and throttle Matt. His silly little comment made her sound vain. Not to mention the sensuous memories dredged up by their privately shared joke. Closing her eyes in an effort to block out the memory, she found herself, instead, reliving it...

Kate opened the expensively wrapped package and pushed aside the snow-white tissue. Inside the folds of paper lay a dress, or at least it appeared to be a dress. Actually, it looked more like a slip, almost to the point of being indecent. Not wanting to disappoint Matt, she donned the flimsy yet undeniably sexy dress and came to stand in front of him. Arms spread wide and raised skyward, she turned in model fashion and smiled vampishly for Matt's imaginary camera. "It clashes with my hair," she pouted with feigned precociousness.

"No, it doesn't. It looks great. Sexy. As a matter of fact, the only thing you'd look better in is nothing at all." He approached her like a wild animal circling its prey. When he took her into his arms, Kate understood exactly why Matt had bought her a dress he knew she'd never wear. Or, at least, not for long.

Damn him for making her remember.

****

Matt wondered what thoughts were going through Kate's head. Judging by the frown on her beautiful face he'd upset her with the crack about her hair.

Do you remember the same things, Kate? When you think about our past, do you remember both the silly and the passionate? Do you react as I do to the memories?

"So, Matthew," Ezekiel asked, drawing him from his thoughts, "what do you think of our world so far?"

"It's all very confusing, of course. And a bit hard to accept. I'm still not certain I believe this is happening. I expect to wake up any minute now and find myself at some stakeout, catching a few minutes shuteye while my partner watches the perps."

"Perps?" Esther repeated in question.

"Perpetrators, crooks, bad guys," Kate explained.

"You will have to excuse my slow-wittedness," Esther explained. "When you live in a world where there is no crime, you have no need for such knowledge."

Both he and Kate pounced on the same key words.

"No crime," they repeated in unison.

"Virtually none," Ezekiel confirmed. "Since any crime, whether it be stealing or worse, is now punishable by death, we have very few problems."

"Death?" Kate repeated. "Even for stealing a loaf of bread?"

"Why would anyone steal a loaf of bread?" Esther asked.

"Maybe they're hungry," Kate suggested.

"It is not possible to be hungry in today's society. The government takes care of everyone. From the time we are born, we are given food and shelter credits. We also receive transportation credits and luxury credits. When we die, any unused credits are given to the beneficiary of our choice."

"And the government pays for all this?" Kate asked.

"It is not really paying, I suppose," Esther explained. "They just give."

"We, in turn," Ezekiel added, "work for either the government-run companies or, as I do, we instruct and guide."

"You're a teacher?" Matt asked.

"I am the equivalent of your early twenty-first

century college professor, I suppose. It is my job to prepare our children for the work-world. Those with high intelligence will go into medicine or will become government elders. Some will become mentors or guides. Those of average intelligence will work in the data storage facilities, or man the three space shuttles we still run between here and the other planets of our galaxy. The remainder work in government-owned factories."

"What do you consider high, medium and low intelligence?" Matt asked.

"No child is born with less than an intelligence threshold of one-hundred fifty. Most average between one-hundred ninety and two-hundred ten. An infant's future is set from the day they are born."

"How do you know what a newborn's threshold will be?" Kate asked.

"Fetal monitoring," Esther explained. "It would be cruel to bear a child of lesser intelligence. There would be no place for it in today's society."

"So you abort a fetus just because it doesn't meet the criteria?"

He had no doubt Kate was taken aback by the comment, the very real emotion sending a flush to her skin, heating her cheeks.

"We look at it as selective parenting," Esther added. "Responsible family planning."

Bitterly, Kate whispered, "It's not selective or responsible anything. It's genocide."

An uncomfortable silence fell across the room. He imagined Kate wanted to apologize. Yet, her emotions were too strong. To say something now would only make matters worse. Silently, she appealed to him.

"Please forgive Kate," he said softly, "the anti-abortion issue is one of her most strident causes."

"It is all right," Esther assured them, "I, too, questioned the validity of the government's decision when I was younger. Now, I understand. I truly believe it would be cruel to sentence a child to a life of hard labor."

"Both of our children," Ezekiel proudly told them, "are medical personnel. Our son travels on the intergalactic shuttle. Our daughter teaches medicine at the academy."

"Academy?" Matt asked.

"The equivalent of your university. Now, they are called academies, mostly because they are run in a military fashion."

"There's certainly a lot to absorb if we're ever going to explain this when we get home," Kate admitted.

Like Kate, he hadn't missed the exchange of glances between Ezekiel and Esther.

"Is there a problem with our reporting our experiences?" Kate asked.

"It is not allowed. When you go back in time, your memories will fade quickly. The more you try to remember, the less will be apparent."

Ezekiel's words explained a lot. That was exactly what had happened when the witnesses had been questioned. The more they had talked, the less the claimants had remembered. There had to be some way to retain everything they were experiencing.

For the sake of Kate's story and his own sanity, there just had to be...

****

"Legally, joined couples never replenish together," Esther told Kate over late-night coffee.

"Replenish?"

"Sleep," Esther explained. "We share a certain amount of time together for pleasure, of course. When we are in our child-bearing prime, we consummate for conception. Otherwise, when we replenish, we lay alone."

"But why?" she asked.

"It is far more efficient. If one cannot sleep, the other is not disturbed. Also, we have privacy, in case we want to be with others."

"Others? You mean adultery is permitted?"

"Adultery? I am sorry, but I do not know what that is?"

"Adultery is when a married person fools around, has sex, cheats on their spouse."

"It is not adultery, Kate," Esther explained. "In our world, you are joined for life for practical purposes. It does not mean you cannot enjoy another person, or their expertise in the pleasures of the body."

"Adultery is probably the leading cause of divorce in our time," Kate explained.

"Is that why you and Matthew divorced? Did you have pleasure with other men?"

"No, of course not."

"Then, did Matthew have other women?"

"No," she said quickly. "He remained faithful right up until the end."

"Then, what happened?"

Kate shook her head, and blinked back the threat of tears, mentally relegating her memories to their allotted corner of her heart.

Esther, wisely, did not pursue the subject.

At energy-replenishment time, she followed Esther into one of the sleeping pods. A square-shaped bed, similar to a child's bunk, hung from the far wall.

"The bathing facilities are through there," Esther explained, nodding toward the seemingly bare wall. Handing the keypad to Kate, she indicated the button on the top left. "Just aim and push."

Kate pointed the remote device toward the wall and pressed the button. Like something from *One*

Thousand and One Arabian Nights, minus the magic words, an invisible door slid upward, revealing a bathroom filled with marble and glass fixtures.

"Hopefully, there is not much difference in the way things work," Esther worried aloud. She then went on to explain, "Everything is a sensor. Nothing to twist or turn, or whatever you do in your time."

"Thank you," Kate said sincerely.

"You are welcome Kate Kelly."

"Brogan," she corrected. "My name is legally—"

"While you are here," Esther interrupted, "you are Kate Kelly." Hesitantly, she added, "It would not be wrong for you and Matthew to spend intimate time together. It would not be—" Esther paused, searching, Kate suspected, for just the right word. "—adultery."

Kate escorted Esther to the door, pleading fatigue. "I'm bushed."

"Bushed?"

"Tired."

Esther nodded knowingly, "Fully expended."

"Yes," she agreed, "fully expended."

"Then, Kate Kelly, I will wish you plentiful and pleasant dreams. If there is anything you wish, you just have to press the third button on the right at the top of the keypad."

"Thanks, I'll remember that."

Esther smiled, and told her, "If you want to say goodnight to your husband, he is on inter-call number six."

****

It would not be wrong for you and Matthew to spend intimate time together.

Kate lay awake long into the night, Esther's words echoing through her head, her thoughts a kaleidoscope of confusion. Why had she been chosen? What, if any, problems did they face in going back? How did couples share a bed barely larger than a child's bunk? How thick *was* the wall separating her and Matt?

She laid her hand against the wall in question, willing herself to feel his presence on the other side. Could he hear the sound of her breathing as vividly as she imagined his? Old memories came flooding back and, with them, the tears Kate couldn't contain.

THREE

Matt woke with a start, his entire body covered with a slick sheen of perspiration. He'd been dreaming. Or, more precisely, he'd been having a nightmare—a nightmare about a botched return to his own time and about never, ever, seeing Kate again.

Rolling onto his side, he stared long and hard at the wall separating him from his ex-wife, and from the remembered pleasure of holding her close. Like an avalanche, the sensations descended upon him, making him ache in places which refused to forget Kate Brogan, no matter how hard he tried.

With a groan, he sat up, his feet hitting the cool floor. When he stood, he bumped his head on the top of the bunk-like bed. Obviously, he thought as he rubbed the sore spot on his forehead, the sleeping quarters weren't designed for a man over six feet.

He lifted the remote from its rechargeable holder and pressed the button Ezekiel had shown him the night before. The door to his right opened and he stepped into the ultra-modern bathroom. Fortunately, facilities hadn't changed all that much in forty-odd years.

****

A voice on the overhead speaker woke Kate from a restless and short sleep; the computerized wake-up call told her that daybreak supplement would be served in thirty minutes.

After a quick shower, she dressed in one of the flowing robes Esther had given her. Mid-calf on almost anyone else, the *simtaki* hung at ankle-length on Kate's diminutive five-foot-two-inch frame. Indigo blue in color, and the most unusual garment she had ever worn, it looked nothing like the futuristic clothes of her sci-fi guided imagination.

Every fold, every pocket, had a function. The belt that cinched the simtaki around her waist had loops for more gadgets than she had in her kitchen junk drawer. The cowl-style neckline lifted into a hood. When not in use, the hood hung like a lightweight collar around the wearer's neck.

After applying a very minimal amount of makeup, and working her shoulder length hair into a neat French braid, Kate felt ready to face the day and the mid twenty-first century.

"So," Matt asked when they were all seated at the table. "What's on the agenda for today?"

"I thought we would begin with a tour outside," Ezekiel informed them. "Provided, of course, you are interested in seeing what has become of the city."

"Very interested," Kate confirmed.

"I should warn you," Ezekiel said, "news of your arrival has spread at ten times the speed of light. You will, undoubtedly, face some intense scrutiny while we are out and about." He paused for a moment and then asked, "Will that bother either of you?"

"No," Matt answered for them both, and she nodded in agreement.

"Good." Motioning toward her half-filled plate, Ezekiel suggested, "Nourish yourself, Kate, and we will be on our way."

Their morning meal over and done with, she and Matt followed Ezekiel to the waiting elevator. "Won't we need coats of some sort?" Matt asked. "After all, it is December."

"Take my word for it," Ezekiel assured them, "you will have no need of an outer covering."

"But—" Matt began, only to stop short when

Ezekiel opened the door and ushered them out into the unusually warm December air.

The moment they stepped out onto the street, Kate recognized her beloved Manhattan. Despite the obvious disparity in seasonal temperature, all the time in the world couldn't make a difference in the way the city felt, especially to a native New Yorker. The air itself crackled with excitement. Everywhere she looked, no matter how much things had changed, she spotted signs of the city she loved so dearly.

The dorm-style building where Ezekiel and Esther lived bordered the water, the edge of Manhattan. The realization prompted her to ask, "Are there still five separate boroughs in New York?"

Ezekiel shook his head. "No, Kate. Beyond what you once knew as Manhattan, there is very little in the way of civilization."

"But, where are all the people?"

Ezekiel sighed deeply, and then motioned for them to come closer. "It is very unclear as to how much of our history I should tell you. We never anticipated having someone visit on an extended basis, and especially not two people. We have no contingency plan for sharing background information."

"Whatever you can tell us," Matt suggested, "will make this whole concept easier to digest."

"Come," Ezekiel said, motioning them forward, "I will tell you as much as I can while we walk."

They'd taken no more than two or three steps when Matt reached for her. Willingly, she placed her hand in his, eager for the warmth of his touch. The moment their hands closed around one another she became engulfed in a flood of memories. Closing her eyes for the briefest of moments she felt a strange sensation wash over her. For some inexplicable reason, she experienced a strong sense of déjà vu, an even stronger bond with her surroundings. The moment Ezekiel spoke, she realized why.

"We are walking through what used to be Battery Park. Over there, to the right, the trees have been replaced by living quarters and one of many government factories. The buildings to the left..."

Ezekiel's generic descriptions echoed in her head, while her mind settled a million miles, or more precisely over forty years away. Matt's hand tightened around hers, the meter of his stroking thumb increasing steadily with each word Ezekiel spoke. She sensed Matt's anger, his disappointment, at the destruction of what used to be a very special place in both their lives.

They'd met right here, eight years earlier. Two years after that, they'd been married in the courthouse just yards from where they now walked. Together, they'd volunteered on a cleanup committee that had repaired and painted signs and fences and historic landmarks. They'd walked and talked, and planned someday to push their baby around the park in a carriage.

Some plans were obviously not meant to be.

Swallowing back the lump forming in her throat, Kate mentally shook herself back to the present—the future—and zeroed in on the sound of Ezekiel's voice.

"...and, over here you will find that we have saved some of the cement work, including one very impressive piece of sculpture."

By the time they reached the harbor, Kate felt awash in barely-concealable regret. Other than a few landmarks, very little of the city remained.

"What happened to Lady Liberty?" she asked.

"The first of three civil disputes," Ezekiel said simply, "in 2026."

"Nuclear bombs?" Matt asked.

"Heavens no. Nuclear bombs were outlawed in

2022, right after the government developed a viable alternative. Nuclear weaponry ruined the entire eastern hemisphere, leaving behind little in the way of people or land. The government was not about to let that happen here, so they destroyed every nuclear device known to man."

"What about the other two *disputes*?" Kate asked.

"The second and third attacks were made by insignificant little armies out to make a name for themselves."

"Kind of like a gunslinger in the old west," she observed.

"I had not thought about it in that context, but I suppose the analogy would fit," Ezekiel agreed. "Our new frontier, as you might describe it, is in many ways like what I have read about the old west. We are a peaceful world, working hard to survive, minding our own business. Then, every decade or so, some unknown military force comes along and tries to kill us off."

"You're right," Matt agreed, "a strange but fitting analogy."

"Strange, yes," Ezekiel echoed, "and accurate. To a degree."

"What's the difference?" Kate asked.

"There is no stepping off twenty paces, no turning and shooting anymore. Attacks are swift and done by computer. There is very little retaliation time. An entire confrontation is over in less than ten minutes."

"In minutes?" She repeated in question.

"How many lives are lost in this confrontation?" Matt asked.

"As many as a million, or as few as a couple hundred thousand," Ezekiel explained. "The incident of 2026 lasted three and half minutes, and wiped out over a million people."

She backpedaled closer to Matt's side. "What happened to the attacking armies?"

"They were defeated, but not without cost to both sides."

She couldn't stop the shiver from running down her back. She swallowed the horrible taste in her mouth when she thought of the destruction of life that seemed so commonplace in this strange new world. Ezekiel's words were too much to comprehend, his matter-of-fact commentary on the destruction of a country, another human being, too cold and calculated to accept.

As if Matt sensed her discomfort, he slipped his arm around her shoulders and drew her close.

Don't let him get to you. Pull away. Save what's left of your heart.

Yet, she couldn't. Not yet. Not until she had to. Not until she and Matt were safely home.

They walked back on the opposite side of the street. In each new sector, as Ezekiel called them, they were introduced to another facet of the future, another anomaly she couldn't accept or understand.

"What's this building?" Matt asked, his gaze lifted skyward.

"This," Ezekiel said proudly, "is the government's headquarters."

"But what about Washington, D.C.?" Kate wondered. "What about the White House and the Pentagon?"

"Perhaps I have not made myself as clear as I should have," Ezekiel admitted.

"Such as?" Matt prompted.

"There is no Washington, D.C. There is no Los Angeles, no Chicago, no Detroit. For all intents and purposes, what you see is all there is in the way of quality of life. New York which, by the way, is only called New York by a few old timers is the focal point of the entire Planet Earth. There are other colonies spread out over what is left of the old states, but none of them have prospered."

"What about other countries?" Kate asked.

"As I said earlier, the eastern hemisphere is non-existent. The western hemisphere exists solely of what is left of Canada and the U.S. Most of Old Canada's land has been turned into wildlife preserves. The upper regions are uninhabitable and overrun by vegetation. Miles and miles of California's coastline fell into the ocean because of a massive earthquake along the San Andreas fault. The desert regions are no longer livable, even at night. With a seventy-five percent loss of the ozone layer, the heat in the desert never gets below one hundred sixty."

She wanted to dispute everything Ezekiel told them. Yet, deep inside, she knew he spoke the truth. Global warming had occurred, just as the scientists had predicted. This, in turn, explained the eighty-five degree temperature in December and the lack of humidity.

"Could we go inside?" Matt asked, his gaze still drawn to the structure housing the government offices.

"No, not without an appointment. I do have top level security clearance but until I get permission we can go no farther than this. Should your return be delayed much longer, I will ask permission for an audience with the president."

They returned to Ezekiel's building, stopping only long enough to supply the electronic sentry with both a fingerprint and voice identification check. Once cleared, they took an elevator to the fifteenth floor, six floors higher than Ezekiel's apartment.

"Where are we?" Matt asked.

"I have brought you to data retrieval. Since I have already told you more than I had intended, I see no harm in letting you review some of the historical archives going back to the current year in which you live."

The thought of exploring things that had, as yet, not happened quickened her pulse, piqued her curiosity. "How do we do that?"

"Take a seat at the console," Ezekiel instructed. "I will explain how the system works."

Once he'd given them basic instructions on the relatively user-friendly data base, Ezekiel explained, "I have some business to attend to. I will have your mid-day supplement brought to you and then come back for you later in the day."

Kate shifted in her seat. "Ezekiel?"

"Yes, Kate, is something wrong?"

"No, but I do have a question about something you said earlier."

"Which is?"

"If New York's not New York anymore, what's it called? And why?"

"When the current government took over, it was decided that a large part of the social problems we were facing stemmed from what was deemed destructive influences, among them a deterioration of our moral values. Although we were an advanced society, some of us were beginning to repeat the mistakes of our ancestors. Our leaders began their planned transformation to a more holistic society by renaming anything and everything that reminded us of the past. They forbid us to choose certain names for our children, claiming they had bad connotations. Then, when they had put every other sanction in place, they eliminated the most obvious and direct link to the past. The city you both know as New York or, more precisely Manhattan, has been renamed Ankara, after the ancient Egyptian city of temples."

Ankara. The city of temples. What other customs had this futuristic society gleaned from ancient civilization?

43

Perhaps the databanks could answer her questions and fill the curious void between what she knew and what she could only imagine.

She and Matt took turns manning the enormous console of the main database while the other used the smaller computer. They began, as Ezekiel had suggested, in their current year.

Kate went directly to the political records, identifying not only the elections, but also the cold wars, the real wars and, ultimately, the end of the world as she knew it.

When it was Matt's turn at the master terminal, he chose human interest stories, sports, and crime details.

"Look at this," Matt commented, pointing his finger at one of the entries. "This has *got* to be a typo."

"Why? What does it say?" She diverted her attention from the data she'd chosen on the government-ordered destruction of the Brooklyn Bridge to Matt.

"*The Yankees win the World Series, ending a decade-long drought to bring the championship back to the United States from Mexico and end that country's ten year domination of the world baseball classic.*"

"Mexico?"

Turning back to the computer screen, Matt added, "Now that's what I call free trade. What are you reading, Cricket?"

"My data screen is a little over a decade old, and right around the time the government started their societal cleanup campaign. It's a recap of the government's attempts to isolate them from the rest of the country by tearing down the bridges leading to and from the island. Listen to this...*In an effort to keep unsavory elements from coming onto the island officials have announced plans to tear down the last*

44

remaining ground link to the mainland. As of Tuesday, March 10th, 2049, the sector-two bridge will be closed to traffic. The mayor's office has confirmed transportation by air and water will continue as usual."

Pausing for barely a heartbeat, she added, "Oh, Matt, this is so hard to believe. How could this have happened?"

****

Matt cut the power to the larger computer. Then, reaching past where Kate sat, he shut down the smaller one too. He'd had enough for one day and he suspected Kate had overloaded on facts as well.

Telltale signs of fatigue shone on her face like a Thespian's greasepaint. Her eyes were shadowed by dark circles, and her cheeks tinted a ruddy shade of pink. Masked in weariness, her usually bright eyes were dull and the whites bloodshot from staring too long at the computer screen.

They needed rest.

A good night's sleep in each other's arms.

A voice inside his head came instantly alive, reminding him that sleeping would likely be the last thing he'd want to do if he ever got Kate in his bed again. Kate had often accused him of having no conscience, but she'd been wrong. Since their divorce, the nasty little beggar had often reared his ugly head to remind him of his mistakes and of how big a jerk he'd been in letting Kate go.

"I'm beat," she said suddenly, pulling Matt back to reality with a jolt.

"Me, too, Crick—Kate," he agreed. "I wonder how much longer we'll have to wait for Ezekiel."

"I don't know, I guess we'll—"

Almost as if he'd been eavesdropping, Ezekiel chose that moment to reappear, coming through the door with another man and a young boy who Matt

45

guessed to be around twelve or thirteen.

"Well, Mr. and Mrs. Kelly," the unknown man said, "have you enjoyed reviewing our databanks?"

"Yes, and no," he admitted honestly. "Some of the information is borderline unbelievable."

"Oh, but it is all the truth, every word of it. You have the government's guarantee."

"You're with the government?" Matt asked. Kate, he noticed, had recovered from her fatigue rather admirably and sat up straight, her chin tilted in its usual obstinate fashion, eagerly awaiting the man's answer.

"I am Peter Westmoreland, President of the United States, and political leader of the planet, Earth."

"It's an honor," Kate said, holding her hand out to the president.

Peter Westmoreland took Kate's offered hand in his and brought her fingertips to his lips. "The pleasure, Mrs. Kelly, is all mine."

If Kate dared to point out to Peter Westmoreland that they were divorced, Matt intended to wrap his hands around her pretty little neck and squeeze. Judging by the man's lascivious grin, the seemingly inherent presidential weakness for beautiful women hadn't changed much in the intervening years.

"Who are you?" Matt asked the boy.

"I am Daniel Westmoreland. My father has asked that I serve as your guide while you are here so that Ezekiel can return to his regular duties."

"I appreciate your offer, but I think we'd fare much better with an adult—"

"Mr. Kelly," Daniel said, his voice stiff with implied insult, "I am a graduate of the academy. Within the next six months, I will be qualified to practice medicine. I feel confident I can handle this assignment as your guide."

"Sorry, Daniel," Matt apologized, "I keep forgetting how advanced society has become. Back where we come from, at your age, a boy's main interests would be playing baseball and chasing girls."

"Baseball is no longer a viable form of entertainment and, contrary to what you might think unsuitable for my age, I already have a match selected for my joining."

"A match?" Kate asked.

"Yes," Daniel explained, "my future life-partner has been chosen for me based on computer data and emotional profile. Sarah must wait until she has graduated the academy before her father will consent to her joining."

"How old is Sarah?" Matt asked.

"She's fifteen, six months my junior."

"Enough, Daniel," President Westmoreland inserted smoothly, his politician's voice polished to perfection. "It is time to show Mr. and Mrs. Kelly to the shuttle car."

"I thought we would be staying with Ezekiel and Esther," Kate said.

"Their job is done. From this point on, you will both be guests of the government and housed at the official residence."

"But—" Matt began only to be interrupted by Ezekiel.

"It is regrettable, Mr. Kelly, but standard protocol for visitors from outside the city, especially visitors of your importance."

Matt sensed Ezekiel's discomfort at being put on the spot and suspected that he had no say in the matter. Nor, it would seem, did he or Kate.

"When will we be able to go home?" He asked, his bluntness intentional, his tone firm.

"Soon," Westmoreland promised. "Ezekiel is working diligently on identifying the return coordinates. Perhaps, by this time tomorrow, our world will be no more than a pleasant dream."

Or, a nightmare, Matt thought to himself. Out loud, he said, "Hopefully."

Matt took hold of Kate's elbow and guided her forward, his other hand held defensively at his side. Daniel led the way, slowing down every so often to identify himself to the security system, stopping only when they'd reached the street.

"Tonight," Daniel told them, "you will dine in the privacy of the guest suite rather than with my father."

"We don't want to be any bother," Kate said.

"It is no bother, Mrs. Kelly."

A motorized golf-style cart waited in front of Ezekiel's building. "Right this way," Daniel instructed, opening the half-door and helping Kate inside.

Matt took the seat at Kate's side, leaving Daniel to sit on the narrow seat next to the driver.

"Your father's not coming with us?" Kate asked.

"No, Mrs. Kelly. He has stayed behind to discuss the details of your return to your time."

At his side, Kate shifted in her seat and leaned forward to be heard above the purr of the cart. "Will Ezekiel be handling the logistics? How long will it take to come up with the correct calculations?"

Turning to face her, Daniel asked, "Are you always so inquisitive, Mrs. Kelly?"

Had the question come from an adult, he had no doubt Kate would have taken immediate offense. Yet, she seemed at a loss as to how she should respond to a boy nearly young enough to be their son.

Matt laughingly explained, "Kate's inquisitive nature is one of her more endearing qualities, Daniel."

"Endearing to whom, Mr. Kelly?"

Me, for one. "Her readers. Kate's won a number of journalistic awards for her investigative reporting. Her inquisitive nature is one of her most reliable research tools."

"In this time and place, Mr. Kelly, it will only get her into trouble."

The drive to the tall, glass-fronted building Ezekiel had shone them earlier took less than five minutes and Matt spent the time studying the streets and buildings around them.

"This building houses both the office and residence?" he asked.

"Yes. The first twenty floors are devoted to offices, data storage, and historical archives. The top ten floors make up the official presidential residence."

After they'd cleared security, Daniel guided them onto the elevator and up to the twenty-fourth floor. Opening the door with nothing more than the touch of his hand, he told them, "This is the guest suite."

"It's very nice," Kate commented.

Matt watched her intently as she turned full circle in the center of the room, her wide-eyed gaze taking in every one of the luxurious amenities.

"The facilities are through there," Daniel said, pointing toward the door to his left. "The sleeping area is to the right. If you'd like to freshen up a bit, there are extra clothes in the locker at the foot of the bed. Everything within the suite of rooms is voice activated."

"Voice activated?" Matt repeated.

"Yes," Daniel explained with a small modicum of impatience, "if you wish the door to open, you stand in front of it and speak your order in a clear, concise voice." Daniel turned to leave, stopping at the last minute to add, "The evening meal will be sent up soon. Please feel free to explore the suite's many comforts until then."

Once Daniel had left the room, Matt asked, "What'll we do now, Cricket?"

"Don't—"

He held up his hands in surrender. "Listen, Kate, this is the weirdest damned situation. Please don't get on my case for something as insignificant as a slip of the tongue."

****

Insignificant? Hardly.

Kate treasured the nickname Matt had bestowed upon her, holding it inside herself with the best of their shared memories. Could he possibly know how often she'd wished to hear that silly little nickname over the past two years? How often she'd wanted him to hold her and keep her nightmares at bay?

"I'm going to do some exploring," she told him.

"Why doesn't that surprise me?"

She ignored the sour remark, choosing instead to try her hand at opening doors. Standing before the first door to the left, she said, "Open."

The door remained closed.

A little louder, she ordered, "Open!"

Again, the door refused to budge.

"Open, darn it!"

Matt's laughter rang out behind her, making her even angrier. She spun around and complained, "Obviously, it's not working."

Matt stepped closer and stared directly at the door. "Open door," he ordered.

Much to her chagrin, the door slid effortlessly upward.

"I'd imagine," Matt told her patiently, "with so many *comforts* within the same room, it might be necessary to address them by name."

Hands firmly planted on her hips, Kate glared straight through him. "It looks as if watching all those late-night sci-fi movies has finally paid off."

"If I remember correctly, Cri...Kate, you didn't exactly change the channel."

"No," she admitted grudgingly, "I didn't, but they certainly didn't prepare me for anything like this."

Turning back to face the open door, she peered inside. As Daniel had said, this door led to the bathroom. The opulently furnished room held a sunken Jacuzzi with gold-plated faucets and inlaid tile. Unbidden, images of she and Matt sharing the intimate tub sprang into her head. Slowly, she backed out the door and let it close behind her.

Matt, in the meantime, had become engrossed in inspecting the contents of the desk drawers.

"Find anything interesting?" she asked.

"Nothing out of the ordinary. A pad of writing paper, an unusual-looking pen."

While Matt rummaged, Kate opened the last door, grateful that the verbal sensors worked on the very first try. Crossing the threshold, she stepped inside the suite's sleeping chamber. Like the room she had slept in last night, a bunk-sized bed hung from the far wall. A second bed, almost identical except for the longer frame, hung head to head with the first. It would seem she and Matt were expected to share sleeping quarters.

In our century, you are still married.

"Whatcha doing?"

Matt's voice, so husky, so sexy, so close, ran over her like a warm, lazy rain.

She motioned toward the two bunks. "I guess we're roomies."

"Does that bother you?"

She shook her head and insisted, "No, of course not. I mean, why should it? After all, it's not like anything's going to happen. I mean—" Kate closed her mouth with a resounding snap, angered that

51

she'd let the thought of sharing close quarters with Matt unnerve her so easily.

Chuckling softly, Matt laid his hands on her shoulders and turned her to face the opposite side of the room. "If I were you," he whispered, scant millimeters from her ear, "I'd worry less about those damned little bunks and a far sight more about *that.*"

She couldn't smother the gasp fast enough, her swift intake of breath drawing another of Matt's sexy chuckles.

Against the opposite wall sat a third bed, this one round, covered in red satin sheets, and surrounded by gauzy netting. Obviously, the decadent piece of furniture was not meant for sleeping, but rather for lovers. Judging by the turned-back comforter and freshly fluffed pillows, she and Matt were expected to take full advantage.

FOUR

Kate paced the length and width of the sitting room, conscious of little more than the fact that Matt slept soundly in the next room. In the *bed*.

"We might as well make it look as if we've used it," he had said, "after all, that's what they expect."

She hadn't missed the purposeful inflection of his voice, or the wagging of his thick dark brows. In defiance and possibly self-defense, she had turned her back on him and stormed out of the room. Now, hours later, she could hear Matt snoring softly, seemingly oblivious to her discomfort.

She was tired. So very, very tired. This totally unexpected flight into the future, along with the stress of all the information she'd tried to ingest, had taken an enormous toll on her inner strength, not to mention taxing her usual reserves.

Yet, when she logically should have been sound asleep, here she stood or, more accurately, paced. She'd tried the sofa, but the ultra-slim styling hurt her back. She needed sleep, yet she couldn't gear down; she couldn't make her thoughts, or her pulse, quit racing. She wanted nothing more than to climb between those red satin sheets and wrap her arms around Matt. Unfortunately, she couldn't follow through, especially knowing how hard it would be to let him go a second time.

Although, it wouldn't hurt, she reasoned, to lay down on one of the bunks. It wouldn't, amend that, *shouldn't* bother her that Matt slept less than a room's length away. After all, they were both mature adults. Weren't they?

"Open door," Kate said softly, careful to not wake Matt. His snoring, she noticed, had stopped. She stood stock still for a moment, listening for the sound of his breathing, disappointed when all she heard was silence.

Tiptoeing across the pitch-black room, she felt for the edge of the bed. When she'd safely reached the bunk, she slipped off the simtaki, letting it fall in a heap at her feet, leaving her standing there in her bra and panties. She spared a single fleeting thought for the gown that hung in the bathroom. She was far too tired to go after it, choosing instead to sleep in the functional cotton of the undergarments Esther had so thoughtfully provided. As a replacement for her own silk and satin, however, they left something to be desired.

After removing her shoes and stockings, she climbed beneath the covers and drew the lightweight sheet up to her chin. Rolling onto her side, she stretched out. Immediately, she came in contact with a hard body. A naked body. Beneath her trembling hands, she felt the power and heat that could come from only one source. One man. Two strong arms surrounded her, drawing her close. Wiry hairs brushed the bare skin of her midriff, tickling her senses. Near her ear, came the hauntingly familiar voice she'd heard often during the past two years, albeit only in her dreams.

"Hi there, sweetheart. I thought you were never coming to bed."

"Matt!" Scrambling from beneath the covers, she shot out into the middle of the room like spent cartridge from an automatic weapon. "I thought you were sleeping in the, ah—" Groaning, she added, "you know what I mean in the—"

"Bed, Kate. The word you're looking for is bed."

"No," she argued, hugging her arms tightly around her scantily clad body, grateful for the darkness. "That's not a bed, that's a—"

"Kate, calm down. You're getting all worked up over nothing. I changed my mind, that's all. The other bed seemed too big without company."

"I'll go back to the sitting room."

"No, Kate. Take the other bunk." After a moment's pause, he added, "You need some sleep, even if it's only for a few hours."

Reluctantly, Kate climbed into the second bunk, the head of which lay less than six inches from Matt's. His arms were stretched out above the bunk, his hands dangling over the edge. If she reached out, she could touch him; if she extended her arm, she could run her fingers through his hair.

"Kate?"

The slow, languorous sound of his voice meant he was, once again, on the verge of sleep. It was a sound she had heard, and loved, often during their marriage. "Hmm."

"I've no intention of hurting you, Kate. I promise I won't do anything—"

"I know, Matt," she interrupted. "It's just all so unusual. I guess I'm a bit on edge that's all. I guess I—" When he didn't answer, she whispered, "Matt?"

Reaching out, she felt for his outstretched hand. Laying her fingers inside his palm, she tucked her thumb around his larger one. It felt right, comforting. Closing her eyes, she willed herself to relax and sleep, thoroughly content when Matt closed his hand tightly around hers.

****

A chime sounded softly above Kate's head. The overhead lights came alive slowly, filling the room with a soft, rosy glow. She drew a hand across her eyes and pushed the hair away from her face. Something seemed wrong, she thought absently. Out of place. She didn't have chimes in her bedroom, and the lights weren't on a timer.

Off in the distance, she could hear Matt engaged in conversation. It always amazed her how comforting she found the deep, even tones of Matt's speech. No matter how frazzled she got, Matt could always calm her.

Anxious to wrap her arms around him and tell him how much she loved him, she pushed the covers off her legs and sat up in the bed, hitting her head in the process.

Bringing her back to her senses.

They weren't at home. They weren't married. Matt would never be there to hold her, comfort her, again.

Slipping into her clothes and then her shoes, she made a second pass of her hand over her hair, shoving the tangled strands aside. In an effort to regain her composure, she drew in a deep breath. Cinching the belt of the simtaki, she stepped through the door and came face to face with Matt and Daniel Westmoreland.

Their conversation, seemingly so involved before, fell silent. Kate felt Matt's penetrating gaze clear through to her soul.

"I just...I mean—" She snapped her mouth shut, angered by her inability to form a coherent sentence. Nodding toward the opposite side of the suite, she hurried off in the direction of the bathroom.

Through the door, Matt called, "Your own clothes are hanging beside the door. Esther laundered everything and sent it over early this morning."

Kate discarded her borrowed wardrobe and stepped beneath the shower, letting the warm water wash over her, through her. When she was thoroughly drenched, she reached for the button which would dispense liquid soap, cleansing cream as Esther had called it. Taking a handful of the thick mixture, she massaged her arms, her neck, her shoulders, spreading the cream over every nook and cranny of her body. Closing her eyes against the anticipated sting of the soap, she couldn't keep her memories from intruding. She couldn't help but remember another time, another shower...

"Move over, Cricket. I'm in a hurry."

Matt slid into the shower stall beside her, his hands coming to rest on her hips. He dipped his head beneath the water, letting the heavy stream run over him like a waterfall amid a hot-water spring. Taking the bar of soap in his hand, he lathered his chest, his broad shoulders, and his long arms. Kate blinked the water from her eyes, watching him; eagerly seeking out the evidence of his thoroughly male body. Putting her hand in his, she stole the soap and his breath, with her very first stroke.

He came alive in her grasp, hardening instantly. The mere thought that she could affect him so easily changed the meter of her breathing, brought her own body to a sudden state of frenzy.

"No, Cricket, don't," he begged, but to her, his voiced lacked sincerity. "I've got an appointment. Kate, baby, don't..."

A loud knock on the glass partition separating the shower from the bathroom proper drew Kate from her memory, her fantasy.

"Yes?"

"Come on, Kate, hurry up. The president's waiting."

****

Breaking the fast with the president—now there was a concept Kate had never imagined. Not in her wildest dreams.

Westmoreland sat at the head of the table, his son and two daughters at his side. His life-mate, Arianna, sat at the opposite end of the huge table, with two of the president's advisors at her side. She and Matt sat in the middle of everything.

"So," Matt asked, "what are the plans for our return?"

Daniel Westmoreland spoke first. "According to our calculations, the best time for your return will be tomorrow morning at six-thirty seven."

"So soon?" Kate wondered aloud, doing her best to hide her mixed emotions.

"Yes, Mrs. Kelly, as soon as possible. It is best that way. The longer you stay, the more powerful your memories will be, and the longer they will take to fade, a fact that could be dangerous for us all."

"Yes," she agreed halfheartedly, "I suppose."

"What would you like to do today?" Mrs. Westmoreland asked. Although her question seemed meant for them both, her gaze held fast to Matt's. "For entertainment, I mean."

Inwardly, Kate fumed. Outwardly, she pretended a calmness she surely didn't feel. Shrugging, she said, "I'm sure whatever you usually do will be fine."

"Usually," the president told her, "we watch video files and listen to the symphony on the data base. We have some wonderful vintage recordings from the late twentieth century."

Kate stifled a laugh behind her napkin.

"Something I have said amuses you, Mrs. Kelly?" the president asked.

"I guess I'm having a hard time thinking of the time I come from as *vintage*."

"If you don't mind," Matt said, "I'd like to look through some more of the historical data files."

"Is there something in particular you are looking for, Matthew?" Mrs. Westmoreland asked.

"Nothing specific," he told her, "I'm just curious."

"If you don't mind," Kate added, "I'd like to go with him."

"Certainly," President Westmoreland agreed,

"I'll have my son escort you back to the records section."

****

Their morning meal complete, they followed their young guide to the data center. Matt was surprised to see Ezekiel busy at work at one of the consoles.

"Hello, Ezekiel," Matt said in greeting.

"Hello, Matthew, Kate. I see you got your clothes back."

"Yes," Kate confirmed, stuffing her hands in the pockets of her casual slacks. "Good-old turn-of-the-century duds."

"Duds?" Ezekiel asked.

"That's slang for clothes," Matt explained.

"Slang. I remember slang. Common, and sometimes crude colloquial sayings, indicative of time and region."

"That's it," Matt confirmed, chuckling, and then asked, "What are you working on now?"

"Your return coordinates."

"I thought Westmoreland said everything was complete."

"He is confident we will have everything in place by the morrow. Our initial figures indicate an early departure would be best. My main concern is at the other end. We have never returned someone without Madame Olga being there to receive them."

"Exactly *where* will we end up?" Kate asked.

"That is the problem."

Warily, Matt asked, "What kind of problem?"

"Well, according to our calculations, you must be sent back to somewhere you have been within the preceding twenty-four hours. Other than at Madame Olga's, you have not been together in that timeframe. Which means, you will be sent back separately. We have never had to deal with something like this. It is all very tenuous."

59

"Why can't we be returned to Madame Olga's?" Matt asked. "Surely she won't be surprised when we land in her parlor?"

"That is another problem, a glitch as you might call it, we had not counted on."

"Glitch?" Kate asked, repeating Ezekiel's excellent attempt at slang.

"It seems the media has gotten hold of the news of your joint disappearance. The police are now involved, and Madame Olga has been closed down and taken into police custody."

"So? The house is still there," Kate pointed out. "Why can't we just *land* in the house?"

Patiently, Ezekiel explained, "The receiving slot in time must be neutral. There must be no chance of interference. We cannot risk being discovered. Currently, Madame Olga's home is overrun by both police and media. There is constant surveillance on the property."

"Why can't we go back to before the transportation?" Matt wondered. "Then your world can ignore Madame Olga's knock on the *door*?"

Ezekiel hesitated for barely a heartbeat but yet the pause was long enough to spike Matt's wariness. "I am not always the receptor. I cannot guarantee the same thing would not happen again."

"But—" Matt began, only to be interrupted by Kate.

"Where else can we go?"

"We had thought of sending you each to your separate homes. Yet, according to our data, you Matthew, have not been home in nearly three days."

"Couldn't I just go to Kate's?"

"Not unless that is where you spent the twenty-four hours."

Ezekiel looked at him expectantly, obviously waiting for his positive confirmation.

Matt raised his hands in defeat and shook his

head. "Sorry."

After a moment's awkward pause, Ezekiel explained, "Then, it looks as if we will have to go with our original plan. One will have to go tomorrow and the other the next day. It would be my suggestion that you go first, Matthew."

"Why him?" Kate asked.

"Matthew will be our test case, so to speak. Once we have confirmed his return, we will send you."

"No! You can't send Matt unless you're positive this is going to work. If there's any chance something could go wrong, then we'll stay here." Turning in his direction, she added, "That is, if you want to."

"You cannot stay," Ezekiel told them emphatically. "Time and time travel are very intricate concepts. You cannot alter the future, or the past, in such a profound way."

Matt reached out and drew Kate to his side, offering his strength as much as he needed hers. Holding her tightly, he said, "Perhaps, you should have thought of that before you let Madame Olga's abilities intrude on your world."

"This did not happen by choice. Her unusual powers threatened our defense barriers. Until we knew what we were dealing with, it seemed easier to let the time travelers in, than to fight to keep them out. It started out harmlessly enough, a bit of ironic humor, perhaps. In some cases, we considered it an experiment of our own. Until you two. Now, we are faced with a problem we never anticipated. And, despite our advanced technology, I am at a loss as to how to deal with it."

"Well, one thing's for sure," Matt told him, "we can't stay here. The little I've read about time continuum indicates any changes in history, no matter how small, can be catastrophic."

"Maybe the two of you have a handle on this,"

Kate added, "but I'm still fuzzy on this continuum thing."

"Come with me," Ezekiel told her, "I will provide you with an example."

He and Kate followed Ezekiel into a second room and, like the other data centers, its walls were lined with computer banks. "What's in here?" Kate asked.

"Twentieth-century birth and life records." Taking a seat at the main console, he admitted, "I had not planned on showing you this but, perhaps, it will help explain the sequence of things."

Eagerly, Matt realized, Kate slipped into the seat at Ezekiel's side. Despite all they'd been through, all the things she should be wary of, Kate's curiosity remained aroused.

Ezekiel played the unusual keyboard like a concert pianist on a baby grand, eliciting from the highly advanced console a series of blips, beeps, and whirs that brought the closest monitor to life. In the first data field, he entered the requested name, Kelly, Matthew. At the second field he paused and asked, "What is your date of birth?"

"October 9, 1983," both he and Kate said in unison.

The computer whirred and bleeped, spitting out the requested information. "Date of birth, parent's names, date of marriage," Ezekiel confirmed.

Ezekiel continued, "Date of divorce. That's funny, it's blank. It shouldn't be." Reading further, he confirmed a number of milestones Matt had yet to experience, including the birth of two children.

Kate's gaze widened and then fell to the floor. What was she thinking? Was she wondering who he would marry? Who might give him another chance at fatherhood? As far as he was concerned, there was no one other than Kate.

"Date of death, none," Ezekiel finished, drawing his attention from Kate and back to the computer screen. "Your record, while not totally accurate, seems to be intact."

"Let's try Kate's information. Date of birth, Kate?" Ezekiel asked.

"April 25, 1986," she told him.

Ezekiel punched in the numbers and then asked, "maiden name?"

"Brogan."

"Okay, we have—" Ezekiel paused.

"What?" Kate asked anxiously, no doubt wondering if Ezekiel had found something horrible in her records.

"There's nothing after your marriage, no record of divorce, no indication of anything after the current year...your current year."

Matt leaned closer to the screen, staring at the same stats Ezekiel had just shared. "How could that be?"

"I am not sure. I will have to run some tests."

"What's your best *guess*?" Kate asked.

"The most logical explanation would be an error in the data input."

"Or?" Matt prompted.

"Possibly, somewhere in the past, part of Kate's life fell into a time warp. An event, most likely traumatic, that never should have happened. We know from studying this type of phenomenon, that occasionally we experience a break in the time continuum which might account for the lack of events. Perhaps, Kate fell into one of those voids. Maybe, for instance, your divorce should have never happened, therefore neither of you show an entry in that field."

Kate brushed her fingertips across the screen. "But, what about the fact that I have no data after our divorce."

"That is where I am confused, other than the possibility of entry error. Although, in all the time I have been working on these programs, I have never seen an error in data entry that was not corrected prior to final data filing. Also, there is this," he said, pointing to the final field. "There should be a symbol here...an *end of file* indicator."

Matt studied the look of concern on Kate's beautiful face and then released a long sigh. "It's got to be a glitch."

"Although it would not account for the lack of a date of divorce, there is one other explanation."

"Which is?" Matt asked, although he wasn't certain he wanted to know.

"There is always the possibility that, during our attempt to return you to own time, you make it and Kate does not."

FIVE

"Could that happen?" Kate asked. "I mean, if I didn't make it home, would I remain here?"

"In all probability," Ezekiel admitted. "Unless, of course, we encountered outside interference."

Matt shifted at Ezekiel's side, his temper rising and his patience dwindling quickly. "Outside interference?"

"From someone with other motives perhaps."

"Motives?" Matt responded in question. "I thought we were sent here by a glitch in Madame Olga's usual five-second carnival ride? What possible motives—"

Nervously, it seemed, Ezekiel interrupted, "Maybe someone from your time arranged with Madame Olga to get rid of you. Or Kate. Would anyone have a reason to want to do that?"

Visions of jailed drug-pushers and crooked politicians sent into hiding by one of Kate's exposes danced like macabre visions in Matt's head.

"This is getting way too bizarre for me," Kate told them, interrupting Matt's thoughts. "I wish I'd never gone to Madame Olga's. I wish—"

"Don't worry, Kate," Matt said consolingly, "I'm not going to let them make a mistake. We either go together, or not at all."

"The government elders would never allow that," Ezekiel explained. "They are insistent that we get you back to your own time as soon as possible."

"Then, I suggest," Matt said firmly, "that you look for a way to send us at the same time."

****

65

That afternoon, she and Matt were entertained by the first lady. They sat through two video files and an hour of symphonies. Never one for art-type films and long, boring opuses, Kate ached for some excitement. Here they were in the mid twenty-first century, and she'd spent nearly four hours with possibly the most boring woman in the entire universe.

Matt's expression, she noticed, changed constantly. One moment, he appeared to be as bored as she. In the next instant, both anger and concern clouded his handsome features. What is he thinking? *Is he as worried as I am about tomorrow's planned return? Most importantly, where had he spent the last three days if not in his own apartment?*

Before she could even begin to assimilate the answers to her multitude of questions, one of the president's aides arrived to escort them to the evening meal. Matt held out his hand and pulled her to her feet, placing his hand protectively at her elbow and escorting her forward.

Ezekiel and Esther were already seated at the table. Westmoreland and his wife seated themselves at opposite ends, leaving two seats to the president's left for her and Matt.

Kate turned to Esther, welcoming her with a smile. "Hello, Esther. I wondered if we'd get to see you again before we left."

"I will be there tomorrow morning," Esther assured her. "It will be my assignment to insure the proper setting of the coordinates."

"Tomorrow morning?" Kate repeated, hating the nervous squeak in her voice.

"It has been decided," President Westmoreland announced, "that you will be allowed to travel together. Ezekiel feels he has come up with a plausible equation."

"Great," Kate said excitedly. "I didn't want to let

Matt go alone."

"You must understand," Ezekiel said solemnly, "there is *no guarantee*. Especially considering you have been here far longer than any of your predecessors. You are...an experiment."

"We trust you," Kate told him. "We know you'd never do anything to intentionally harm us."

Ezekiel met her gaze, his dark eyes flaring before his lids closed. "I am humbled by your confidence, Mrs. Kelly."

****

On orders from the president, Ezekiel made his way to Westmoreland's private office. After being announced, he stepped through the door and waited while it slid closed behind him.

"So, Ezekiel, tell me," Peter Westmoreland asked from behind the massive glass desk, "exactly what are your chances of returning Mr. and Mrs. Kelly to their own time?"

"Very good, Mr. President. Surprisingly, the data was not nearly as difficult to retrieve as I had first thought."

"And, you are certain they will have no recollection of what they have seen?"

"As with the others, their memories will fade quickly."

"I would prefer that they fade during transport. Even the smallest memory could endanger us." As an afterthought, Westmoreland added, "Also, this medium, Madame Olga, must be stopped. We can no longer allow her to practice her craft."

"How do you propose to stop her?" Ezekiel asked.

"I am not sure, at this point. My advisors are looking into it."

Ezekiel shifted nervously from one foot to the next, wary of the implication of the president's words. "Where are Mr. and Mrs. Kelly now?"

"Daniel has taken them to their quarters for the night. Arianna has arranged for late night cocktails that will ensure them a good night's sleep."

Unbelievingly, Ezekiel asked, "You are going to drug them?"

"No, not exactly."

"I do not think—" Ezekiel began, only to be sharply interrupted.

"That is correct, Ezekiel. You compute, the government thinks. Is that understood?"

"Yes, sir."

"Good. You are excused. I will expect your return one hour prior to scheduled transport. We will use the central processing computer."

"The central processor? But we have not used—"

"Must I repeat myself, Ezekiel? You are excused."

****

Staring out the suite's largest window, Kate had a clear view of the harbor. The sun had gone down nearly an hour earlier and, off in the distance, a solitary boat, more of a hovercraft, patrolled the shoreline. Farther out, the darkened ruins of the Statue of Liberty stood out like a beacon, its very presence sending a tremor of trepidation down her spine.

Lost in her thoughts, she barely heard the faint tapping at the door. A second round of tapping ended with the opening of the door. Turning full circle, she greeted her visitor.

"Mrs. Westmoreland."

Arianna Westmoreland, looking every bit the regal female counterpart to the most important man on planet earth, stepped into the suite. "Mrs. Kelly," the woman rejoined. "Where is your husband?"

For the first time, Kate noticed the tray the first lady carried in her hands. Her attention drawn to the crystal flutes and bottle of wine, she absently said, "He's in the shower."

The First Lady's gaze flared, changing the color of her eyes from a non-blue to an almost perfect sapphire. "Your husband is a very handsome man, Mrs. Kelly."

"Yes," Kate agreed without hesitation, "he is."

"Esther tells me, where you come from, there is no allowance for reciprocal pleasure. That, in your time, joined couples do not copulate with anyone other than their mates. Is this so?"

"Yes," Kate said firmly, resolutely. "Well, at least that's the way it is supposed to be. Not everyone remains faithful."

"Have you never wanted another man? Or, your husband another woman?"

"I can't speak for Matthew, but I assure you, he's the only man I've ever loved."

"And, even though you are not together in your world, you still love him?"

"I'd rather not talk about this, if you don't mind. My life and Matthew's is no one's business but our own."

Arianna inhaled deeply, straightening her shoulders and assuming a very proper posture. Her gaze flared once more. But, rather than in excitement as before, it now showed impatience.

"I am only trying to ascertain your feelings so that I might ask your indulgence."

"My indulgence?"

"Yes, I find I am quite drawn to your husband. I would like to have pleasure with him this evening. Of course, I would only do so with your permission."

Kate swallowed. Hard. The import of Arianna Westmoreland's words sank into her heart with lightning speed, leaving her dizzy, angry, and, hopelessly jealous.

"You, in turn," Arianna continued, "would be quite welcome to spend an evening with my husband." At Kate's obvious gasp, Arianna added, "It is not many women who can say they have made love with the President of the United States."

That's what you think. Kate let the uncharitable thought pass. "I am sorry, Mrs. Westmoreland, but I have no desire to spend time with the president and, as for Matthew's desires, you'll have to—"

"No, thank you," Matt said from across the room. Fresh from his shower, he stood in the doorway wrapped in a towel, his hair damp and finger-combed into obedience.

"It is a shame, Matthew," Arianna said in resignation. "We could have had a very interesting time." Nodding toward the bottle of wine, she told them both, "In any case, I have brought you some wine and a late day supplement."

"Thank you," Matt said.

"Yes," Kate echoed, "thank you."

Mrs. Westmoreland left them shortly thereafter, bidding them a good sleep and assuring them she would be there to see them off in the morning.

"She makes it sound like we're going on a cruise," Kate grumbled when the door had shut between them and their guest.

"Don't be so hard on her, Cricket. She knows as little about our moral standards as we do about theirs."

"She's a very beautiful woman."

Matt shrugged, his broad shoulders lifting and falling in an even rhythm that drew her gaze. His chest, bare and lightly haired, begged for her thorough inspection. When her gaze dropped to the towel at his hips, she knew she would be lost if she didn't look away.

"Kate," he whispered.

Self-consciously, she turned her back on him, pretending a renewed interest in the view that lay beyond the window. "I think I'll have a glass of the wine. How about you?"

"Sure."

She poured two glasses of wine and then cautiously took a sip. Sweet and dry, the cool liquid slid effortlessly down her throat, relaxing her as it went.

"It's your turn in the shower," Matt reminded her.

"Yes, I guess it is."

"There's a robe and a gown-looking thing hanging in the dressing room."

Finishing off her wine, she set the glass aside and raised herself from the seat she'd taken on the sofa.

"Shall I pour you another for after your shower?" Matt asked, refilling his own glass as he spoke.

"It is rather good, isn't it?" He nodded, and she told him, "Okay, but just half a glass."

When Kate emerged from the bathroom, she found Matt stretched out in front of the video screen.

"What are you watching?"

"I'm not sure. I found the tape in the desk drawer. Someone must have put it there earlier today. I don't remember seeing it last night."

Kate settled herself on the sofa beside Matt and he handed her another flute of wine. Turning toward the monitor, she studied the unusual shapes and colors of the random pattern.

"It looks like something Picasso might have painted on a bad day," she joked.

Reaching out, Matt playfully ruffled her hair, and wrapped one long strand around his finger. "I never realized you were an art critic."

"Not me. If it's not a landscape or wildlife, I'm not interested."

"What do you make of this?" he asked, pointing toward the screen.

"I'm not sure," she confessed. "I don't find it

interesting, yet, for some reason, I feel almost compelled to watch."

"More wine?" he asked.

"Yes, please," she said absently, her gaze drawn unflinchingly to the myriad of changing images on the video monitor.

****

Like Kate, he was having a difficult time understanding the patterns of color and shape. Twice, he'd opened his mouth to order the video screen off. Yet, the shapes and colors had changed suddenly and he'd been intrigued all over again.

At his side, Kate seemed equally enthralled with the visual display. Between them, they'd nearly drained the bottle of wine.

"Last glass," Kate said softly, filling both their flutes to the brim.

Despite the fact that she'd consumed nearly half the wine, she appeared to be perfectly sober. As for his half, he felt no different than when they'd began. Except, perhaps, for a bit of lethargy, he felt perfectly fine. Almost as if it were orchestrated, the videotape ended just as they finished the bottle.

"Monitor off," Kate ordered, her voice husky and infinitely sexy, sinking into his senses as warmly as the wine.

"I think we'd better hit the sack," he suggested. "We wouldn't want to miss our own bon voyage."

****

"Kate," Matt whispered. "Kate, are you awake?"

From the opposite bed, Kate mumbled a vague reply. Slipping out of his own bunk, he stood beside Kate's bed. Beneath the lightweight sheet, the outline of her curves were obvious, even in the darkened room. Reaching out, he touched his fingertips to the smooth slope of her throat, testing the strength of her pulse. Warm to the touch, her satin-soft skin, made his fingers itch. Closing his eyes, he drew a deep breath and tasted the heady flavor of the wine, its distinctive and fragrant bouquet filling his head with sensual thoughts. The pictures his mind conjured up were both colorful and sensual, making him dizzy and powerful at the same time.

Slowly, he peeled back the sheet and slipped into the bed, leaving nothing but Kate's gown between them. Reaching out, he grasped the gown's hem in his hands and eased it upward. Unsure of what drove him, he only knew he needed Kate with a fierceness he'd never experienced before, not even during the most tumultuous days of their marriage. Rather than resist, as he'd expected, Kate curled toward him, wrapping her arms around his neck and snuggling into his grasp.

****

Kate felt herself being lifted and carried, surrounded by a pair of strong arms. She tried opening her eyes. Yet, from somewhere deep within came a voice telling her to let go; relax; enjoy. She licked her lips and tasted the exquisite flavor of the wine. As soon as she thought of the wine, she remembered the video and the kaleidoscope of colors and shapes. They spun again, an instant replay inside her head, showing themselves in unorganized confusion, breaking up and reforming again into intricate patterns.

The cool abrasion of silk sheets beneath her bare skin went through her like ice cubes down a person's back, making her shiver. Warm hands soothed her, touched her, coaxed her into restiveness.

She ached, from the inside out, possessed with a yearning so strong that tears welled up behind her closed eyelids and spilled out through her lashes. His lips were there, sipping up the fallen tears, dusting her face with butterfly kisses, easing the tingling she felt from head to toe.

The kiss seemed natural, inevitable and their mouths mixed and mingled, sharing heat and the sweet hint of the wine.

Crazy. God, she must be crazy! Matt's hands, familiar hands, were everywhere, stroking her, soothing her, bringing her to the brink of fulfillment only to stop short of their ultimate goal.

"Matt," she cried, yet the sound never made it past her lips. Reaching out blindly, she grasped his face in the palms of her hands and threaded her fingertips through his hair, drawing him closer.

Their lips met, a tentative, tender kiss meant to soothe. Willingly, hungrily, she opened her mouth and he thrust his tongue inside, tasting her, stealing her breath, staking his sensual claim. She sought Matt's unique flavor, yet the taste of the wine coated her tongue and filled her mouth.

She needed to see him! Yet, all she could see were those damned colors and patterns. "Matt," she called out again, and again she heard nothing.

He slid down her body, touching, stroking, kissing his way from her head to her toes and back again. The pleasure felt more intense than anything she could remember. She could feel every stroke, every kiss, every brush of Matt's day-old beard against her bare skin as if her body had been sensitized so keenly that it reacted to even the slightest hint of his touch.

She knew she'd hate herself, and him, in the morning, but right at the moment nothing mattered but receiving and giving pleasure. Smoothly, quickly, she turned the tables, rolling Matt onto his back and charting her own course for seduction. She kissed his brow, his forehead, the perfect dimple in his left cheek. When she slid even lower, she felt his groan rather than heard it. When she took him into her mouth, he arched his back and presented himself for their mutual pleasure.

More daring than she'd ever been before, she kissed her way back to his mouth and lifted herself above him, straddling his hips and settling herself in place to receive him. With the very first thrust of his hips, Kate climaxed, crying out until her voice could be heard. Matt groaned, the deep, throaty sound penetrating the thick fog enclosing her.

In a rhythm as old and perfect as time and yet uniquely their own, she moved over him, taunting and teasing, sitting up, arching her back, taking him in until he could go no farther.

"Kate," he whispered, and the single word seemed to release her from the silence and darkness. She opened her eyes and looked down into Matt's face.

His eyes were wide open, watching her as she watched him. Silently, he pleaded with her to forgive him. Yet, when she might have stopped this insane ride they'd taken, he grasped her hips and clenched his hands tightly against her, digging into her flesh, urging her on, begging her to continue, to finish.

He needn't worry. She had no choice. She needed this as much as he did, if not more. When, at last, they reached the very edge of insanity, they both cried out in mixed words of ecstasy, knowing intimately a pleasure-pain neither of them was likely to forget.

Kate collapsed onto Matt's chest, her heart hammering and her breathing as labored as if she'd run a marathon. Matt enclosed her in a tight embrace and rolled onto his side, taking her with him, wrapping them in the silk sheets and sensual heat.

Matt pulled Kate in close to his chest and rested his chin atop her head, her silky curls tickling his skin. In the morning, Kate would undoubtedly regret what they'd done and, rightfully, she'd blame him. She'd never believe he couldn't help himself. That he hadn't been able to control the urge that drove him to seduce her.

Hell, he didn't believe it himself.

****

"Okay, let me get this straight," Matt said impatiently, delving his fingers through his hair. "For some reason I *still don't understand*, we can't go back to Madame Olga's. We can't just be dropped there five minutes before we left."

"Basically, although crudely put, that is true," Ezekiel confirmed.

"One more time," Matt entreated, "explain it to me one more time."

Kate shifted restlessly from one foot to the other, her attention tuned into Ezekiel's words while her gaze rested nervously on Matt.

Memories of their lovemaking came back to her in sudden flashes of light, illuminating her mind like a Friday night in Times Square. She'd...they'd...never made love like last night. It had been erotic, sexual in every sense of the word and, despite the fact that she woke up filled with regrets, she had to admit she'd enjoyed every moment.

Blinking away images which refused to fade, she listened, one more time, to Ezekiel's explanation.

"A person's lifetime is nothing more than a large grid, a huge book of graph paper. Each day is a separate sheet of paper and the very first square represents the beginning of the day, the moment you awake from your replenishment. As the day progresses, you move from square to square. Imagine each square as being an increment of time. Each event within the day begins at the corner of a square. If we could pinpoint the exact *square* in which to return you, you would still have to replay that section of time over again. You would still end up here."

"We could do that," she insisted, crossing the room to stand at Matt's side. "We could go back to the beginning of the square and then you could just let go of my hand."

"I wish it were that simple," Ezekiel admitted. "Yet, when you and Matthew came together through the time warp, you eliminated that possibility."

"How?" Matt asked.

"You were each in different *squares* of your day. Since you had not been together prior to your visit to Madame Olga's, you began your day at different times and your grids do not match. If we were to return Kate to the séance, you, Matthew, would end up somewhere else entirely."

"What, then, is the final plan?" Matt asked.

"We are going to send you back to the beginning of your day. Kate, you will awaken in your bed. You will go to work and live through the day as you would have previously. Matt will do the same. You will meet again at Madame Olga's and you will sit through the séance. The difference, of course, will be that no one will come to get you."

President and Mrs. Westmoreland arrived moments later, and Kate left Ezekiel and Matt to discuss the details of their time trip while she went to greet the first lady.

"Mrs. Westmoreland," Kate said sweetly, hoping her smile looked more natural than it felt, "could I speak with you a moment?"

"Surely, Mrs. Kelly," Arianna replied. "I trust you and Mr. Kelly slept well."

"We barely slept at all," Kate confided. "Although, I'm sure you knew that already. Didn't you?"

"Let us just say, the bottle of nectar and video file were not intended for you."

"You were going to use them to seduce my husband."

"Yes," Arianna admitted. "The mild drug in the nectar, along with the subliminal messages of the video file are a potent combination. I have never known them to fail."

"Is it necessary to drug your sexual partners to have fulfillment in this century?" Kate asked bluntly.

"No, not usually. We use the enhancements only when we wish to have totally uninhibited encounters, free from time or duty constraints. Unfortunately, because of his position of power, my husband is not permitted to let himself indulge. With him, it is controlled and analytical. Uninspired."

The bitterness in Arianna's voice spoke eloquently of her needs, and of her loneliness. Kate felt sorry for the woman. Yet, not so much that she would have wanted Matt to share Arianna's bed.

"It is time," Esther announced, stepping between Kate and Arianna. "Ezekiel has set the coordinates and we are running one last test on the main computer."

"Another test?" Kate questioned. "Ezekiel has already run a half-dozen."

"We have not used this computer in quite some time," Esther explained. "Other than connecting and disconnecting the building's power sources, *Ramses*, has had little to do for over a decade."

"Ramses?" Kate repeated.

"In a decade?" Matt said at the same time. Coming up behind her, he laid his hands gently on her shoulders.

"Ramses is the computer's identitech code. And yes, Matthew, a decade is a very, very long time."

"If *Ramses* is so outdated, why are we using it for the transportation?" Kate asked.

"President Westmoreland believes that, although Ramses is old, it is still the most powerful of the computers. The president's advisors seem to think that power will be the solution to a successful transport, considering the payload is double the usual."

Taking hold of Esther's hand, Kate squeezed, and admitted, "I'm not going to deny that I'm scared to death. What if something goes wrong?"

"It is a risk you must take. You cannot stay here. Mara has seen only trouble for you here."

"Mara?"

"She is Analog Station Three's spiritualist."

"I don't suppose she's any relation to—"

"Kate, it's time to go." Matt's timely interruption drew Kate from her nervous attempt at humor.

"I'm ready. I guess."

Ezekiel placed Kate, and then Matt, on separate platforms in the middle of the room. A dome-like shield came down and covered her from head to waist. A similar device covered Matt, as well.

"What we will be doing," Ezekiel explained carefully, "is to neutralize the air around you, separating the molecules in your body until you disappear into thin air, reappearing again at the set coordinates."

"Is this going to hurt?" Kate asked.

"No," Esther assured her, "you will not feel a thing."

Ezekiel held his hand above the keyboard, his finger poised over but not touching the single key that would send them back home. "Good bye, Matthew and Kate Kelly," Ezekiel said. "Good luck."

****

Matt opened his eyes, his vision focusing on the only thing that mattered, the empty platform where Kate had been. Confusion ran rampant through the room. Ezekiel and Daniel Westmoreland were arguing, their voices rising above the rest.

"What happened?" Matt asked as soon as the

shield lifted.

"I am not sure," Ezekiel said truthfully. "You should have both gone. The coordinates were logged in and the power settings confirmed. Yet, only one pod activated."

"Did Kate make it home safely?"

"That we have not determined as yet," Ezekiel admitted.

Ezekiel had no sooner spoken when Esther came to his side. "The transport confirmation data is in," she stated. "Kate did not reach the set coordinates."

Matt leaned over Ezekiel's shoulder, watching with fervid interest while Ezekiel ran a second and then third set of tests on the results of the transportation.

"Where is she?" Matt asked when he could wait no longer.

Ezekiel shook his head. "I am not sure. All I have been able to confirm is that she did not reach the set destination."

"Is there anything you can do to find her? Can you get her back?"

"I have set return coordinates and have turned the scanners on. If Kate is anywhere within our range, the tractor beam should pull her back."

"And, if she's not?" Matt asked.

"She will be lost to us forever."

SIX

Kate rolled onto her side, tucked her arm beneath her cheek and snuggled into the scratchy straw.

Straw?

Sitting up quickly, she opened her eyes and blinked once, twice. Still, she couldn't make out her surroundings in the dim light. Where the heck was she? More importantly, how had she gotten there?

Strange voices came at her from all sides. She couldn't hear their exact words although they had a very distinct drawl. Southern, perhaps...western, maybe.

She felt her way around in the dark, using her outstretched hands to keep from bumping into anything or anyone. If the pungent aroma of her surroundings were any indication, she'd somehow fallen asleep in a stable or a barn. But how? When?

Slowly but surely, she made her way to the closest door. Anxious, yet apprehensive about what she might find on the other side, she eased the door open and looked out onto the street.

Directly across from her, a horse stood tethered to a hitching post. Buildings made of rough-hewn wood lined either side of the dusty, unpaved road. The tinny sound of a piano crept from beneath the swinging doors of a nearby saloon.

Saloon?

A distinct shiver shimmied up her back. Turning slowly, she surveyed the remainder of her surroundings. A bank, a hotel, McGreevy's Mercantile. At the end of the street, two men stood face to face, their outstretched hands poised above gun holsters. She could easily imagine the twitch of their fingers as they readied themselves for the draw.

There is no stepping off twenty paces, no...

The strange thought, unknown and unfinished, swept through her head, leaving as quickly as it came.

The man with his back to her drew first. The second man responded. They fired simultaneously, yet only one man fell.

She screamed out in terror, belatedly shoving her fist in her mouth to muffle the involuntary response.

"There, by the barn," someone shouted. "I heard something! It must be that other bank robber. Come on, boys. Let's get 'im."

Frantically, Kate scrambled through the barn door, stubbing her toe on a nearby bale of hay. Pain shot up her leg, bringing tears to her eyes and a number of unladylike phrases to her lips. The door of the barn opened behind her.

She ran for all she was worth, through the length of the barn and out a small door in the back. Tripping over the tall grass behind the ancient-looking building, she landed on her hands and knees in the dirt. Pushing herself to her feet, she fled toward a stand of trees off in the distance. Behind her, the door opened and shut repeatedly. Men's voices, raised in angry shouts, filled her head.

"Hang the bastard!" one shouted.

"Damned thievin' bank robbers!" another added.

"Don't let the bastard get to the woods if you can help it!"

Despite the ache in her foot, the pounding of her heart, and the burning in her lungs, she kept running. Bursting through the first row of trees, she reached deep inside herself for one last shot of adrenaline, certain that if she stopped running she'd never come out of the woods alive.

She crouched beneath a flowering bush and drew its long, pliant limbs around her like a cloak. In the distance, she could hear the men's voices, the repeated demands of 'catch the thievin' bastard!', 'hang him from Binkley's oak.'

What's happening? Where am I? Please, please, let this be a bad dream...

Strange visions crept into her head. Bright lights. Tall silver walls.

Matt...

The men came closer, the sound of their approach louder and more menacing with each passing second. Through the thin foliage, she could see four pairs of legs. Denim clad, the legs ended in hand-tooled boots complete with spurs.

Spurs? If this is a dream, it's getting weirder by the moment.

Kate held her breath and issued a prayer for her safety. The men moved on, venturing farther into the woods. She slipped from beneath the bush. Her back ached and her toe throbbed. If she could only get back to the safety of the barn, maybe then she'd wake up. Maybe then this horrible nightmare would end.

Cautiously, she stepped from between the last of the trees and into the clearing. She scanned the horizon, looking for something familiar.

Familiar? That's a stretch. What could possibly be familiar about a time and place she knew nothing about? A place fashioned in an obvious nightmare?

Again the strange vision of lights and sleek walls intruded on her subconscious. Looking for the dilapidated barn she'd run from earlier, she ventured farther into the clearing. She'd taken no more than a dozen steps when she suddenly felt dizzy. An invisible force seemed to be pulling on her, tugging her upward.

From behind her, she heard a gruff voice say, "Well, well, well. What have we here?" A meaty hand closed around her wrist, grounding her. "I'll be damned," the voice continued. "The posse's looking for another man. Not a half-pint woman."

Relying on nothing more than her instincts, Kate pulled her leg back and kicked the man in the shin with her good foot, taking her captor by surprise. Then, breaking free of his hold, she ran out into the middle of the open field, the man in hot pursuit.

"Stop!" the man shouted.

She had no intention of stopping.

"Dammit, girlie, don't make me hafta use force."

No matter how fast she ran, the horrid man kept up with her. Just as he made a grab for her arm, she tripped, tumbling head over heels into the high grass of the open field. The dizziness returned full force.

The man cursed. "I didn't wanna do this—"

The sound of a firecracker, or possibly a car backfiring, echoed through her head. She wrapped her arms around her middle and doubled over in pain. A burning sensation worked its way up her side. Darkness surrounded her and she wondered if she were dead. If not for the spinning of her head, and the incredible pain, she would have thought it quite possible. The sensation of floating upward came back to her full force. Maybe she had died and was now on her way to heaven. Closing her eyes, she accepted oblivion for what it promised: relief.

****

"Dammit, Ezekiel, do something!" Matt's angry demand echoed through the cavernous room, drawing Ezekiel's patient retort.

"Matthew, it will do Kate no good for you to lose your temper."

"Just, exactly, what will do Kate some good?"

"I am doing everything humanly possible to track Kate's whereabouts. For the time being, we must assume she made it to the correct time, if not the correct destination."

"What went wrong? Why didn't I go, too?"

"It would appear," Esther began in explanation, "that Ramses could not handle the power load for a dual transportation. So, being his usual, logical self, he decided to take the lesser of the two payloads."

"*Good-old Ramses.*"

"Sarcasm will not help Kate, either," Ezekiel pointed out.

The urge to throttle someone—anyone—forced Matt to clench his hands into fists at his sides. He felt helpless, useless. Much the same as he had the night Kate had lost their baby. Months afterward, his obsession with finding the person responsible for his baby's murder had finally taken its toll on their marriage.

The thought of Kate hurtling through time and space and ending up who knows where only added to his feeling of helplessness. The thought of never seeing Kate again reminded him of how wonderful it had felt to hold her, kiss her...love her. Not for the first time since they'd begun this god-forsaken day he wished for another few hours in Kate's embrace.

He wished—

"Matthew!" Esther's urgent call drew Matt from his memories.

"Yeah?"

"We have picked up something on the screen. It might be nothing, and then again—"

"It might be Kate."

"Do not get your hopes up," Ezekiel reminded him. "Often anomalies appear—"

"Look!" Esther interrupted, pointing toward the transporter pod from which Kate had departed.

Matt rushed forward, only to be stopped by Ezekiel's restraining hand. "Wait! We cannot touch her until the transport is complete."

Once the audible whir of the transporter pod had stopped, he moved closer, followed by Esther and then Ezekiel.

Kate lay on her back, her eyes closed and her features pinched as if she were in an enormous amount of pain. Matt's gut tightened. Carefully, he reached for her, lifting her into his arms. Something warm and wet coated his hand. Drawing Kate closely to his chest and holding her to him with one arm, he raised his hand for a closer look.

Blood coated his fingers, thick and red. Kate's blood.

"She's hurt," he said automatically, unnecessarily.

Esther examined Kate's back while Matt held her tightly to his chest.

"It looks like a wound from some sort of a primitive weapon," Esther explained.

"A knife?" he asked.

Ezekiel examined the hole in Kate's back more closely, and concluded, "No, not a knife. Kate has been shot."

Matt followed Esther's lead, down first one corridor and then another until they'd reached a large, sterile-looking room. The sentry who admitted them spoke quickly to Ezekiel and then into the small transmitter attached to his collar. By the time Matt placed Kate on the closest bed, medical help had arrived.

"Gunshot wound to the lower left quadrant of the back, torn muscle tissue. The bullet is lodged approximately two inches inside the wound, caught on the outside of the abdominal wall." The doctor's matter-of-fact pronouncements reminded him of his brother Jim, and of another time...another hospital.

His gut twisted. Tears filled his eyes. "Is she going to be all right?"

"I have not seen a wound of this sort in a good number of years," the doctor confessed. "I doubt any of my staff have ever seen a wound made from a handgun. Still, the patient appears to be in no grave danger, other than the possible loss of blood. We will start her on supplemental internal fluid replacement and, then, when she is stabilized, I will remove the foreign object."

"Supplemental internal fluid? You mean blood, right?" Matt questioned.

"We do not store blood the way it was done in your time," Ezekiel explained. "Learned scientists found it to be far too dangerous. Screening procedures were not always foolproof, resulting in tainted blood."

"Now," Esther continued, "we use a fluid replacement similar in chemical makeup to blood, but far more efficient and sterile."

Nearly two hours passed and, to Matt, Kate looked as if she were getting worse instead of better. Her features, dull before, were now a deathly ashen. "Kate," he whispered softly, willing her to hear him. "Kate, baby, hold on. Please."

The doctor reappeared moments later with another, younger, man at his side. Behind them, two women carried a small machine that appeared to be some sort of monitoring device and a tray filled with medical instruments. Apparently, some things hadn't changed, for Matt recognized the forceps, scissors and suture equipment available back at home.

"Place the patient on her stomach," the doctor instructed. "Uncover the wound and sterilize."

"Aren't you going to take her to the operating room or something?" Matt asked. "What about scrubbing up?"

"Operating room?" one of the young women questioned.

"Scrubbing up?" the other asked.

"In the nineteenth and twentieth centuries and on into the twenty-first, I suppose," the doctor told them, "all procedures which required internal probing took place in sterile rooms known as *operating rooms*." Glancing in Matt's direction, he admitted, "I am not sure of the expression, *scrubbing up*."

"That's when you wash your hands and put on sterile, protective gloves before beginning the operation."

"But we did sterilize ourselves," the young man said, "just before we came in here."

"Yes, we did," the doctor agreed, and then explained, "In our time, we walk through a laser field which sterilizes everything, from head to toe, including the clothes we wear."

"Fine," he conceded, eager for them to get on with saving Kate's life.

"You will have to leave," woman number one told him. "You have not been disinfected."

Reluctantly, Matt left the room, taking up a vigil at the door. Through the small port-hole-type window, he could watch the entire procedure which took all of ten minutes. The metallic clink of the bullet being placed on the nearby tray echoed through the room and out into the corridor.

"Well?" he asked when the doctor approached. "Is Kate going to be okay?"

"Yes, Mr. Kelly. Your wife is a strong woman. She has accepted our treatment extremely well. I expect she will be awake any time now."

"Thank you." Relief washed through him. "What about the bullet?" he asked.

"Very large and very primitive. I have not seen too many bullets, as I said before, and never anything quite like this. Perhaps, with your background in law enforcement, you could identify this projectile for me."

The doctor handed Matt the bullet and he rolled it over and over in his palm, and then lifted it to the light.

"Forty-five caliber, roughly made. The gun this bullet came from was old, with a long barrel. These etchings could be someone's initials. Often, when people made their own bullets, they monogrammed them. It looks like a Y or a W and the second letter is definitely an E, and—"

"Excuse me, Matthew," Ezekiel said, his approach drawing both men's attention.

"What is it?" Matt asked, "What have you found out?"

"According to the data we have retrieved from the transport pod's recorder, Kate went all the way back to 1880 and landed in Tombstone, Arizona."

Matt glanced quickly at the bullet in his hand and then back at Ezekiel. "Tombstone, Arizona, 1880?"

"Yes, that is what our data confirms. Is there some significance to that time and place?"

"It's just a hunch, but I'd say somehow, someway, Kate managed to get herself shot by the legendary Wyatt Earp." Inwardly, Matt chuckled to himself, his internal show of emotion the first bright spot in a horrendous day. Leave it to Kate, he thought, to get on the wrong side of one of the world's most notorious lawmen.

****

"Well, Cricket," Matt teased, his use of her nickname blatantly intentional, "what've you got to say for yourself this time?"

"It's not my fault," she argued. "Besides," she said defiantly, "how do I know you're not just making this all up. Wyatt Earp, for heaven's sake.

Just how gullible do you think I am, Matthew Kelly?"

Obviously enjoying every minute of her uncertainty, he stretched out his hand and unfolded his fingers. The bullet lay in his palm. "Look at it for yourself," he encouraged. When she took the bullet from his hand, he added, "Here, take this magnifying glass and look real close."

Kate took her time examining the bullet in question, turning it over and over in her fingers, studying it from every possible angle.

Wyatt Earp. The idea totally boggled her mind. Had she really stumbled onto one of the most famous lawmen in history? The possibilities for a story were endless. If she could only get back to her computer, to the newsroom. If only—

"It doesn't matter. Does it? I mean who, but you and the people here, would believe what happened?"

"We can take the bullet back with us and have it authenticated," Matt suggested.

"What good would that do? You know what Ezekiel told us, we'll not remember we were even here. How can we expect to remember what happened, and where the bullet came from?"

"I think you're putting the cart before the horse, Kate. If we plan it right, we can take some of this back with us."

"But how?"

"We'll write things down. A journal, maybe. Then, when the time comes, we'll take it with us."

Kate lay silent for a moment, her head spinning with the possibilities. Then a thought came to her, sudden and uncontrollable. "What if they never get it right? What if we never get back?"

Matt gathered her hand in his and pressed her palm to his lips. She thought of pulling away, but the warmth of Matt's touch and the sweetness of his kiss enticed her into ignoring their problems, their differences. For now, and until they were safely back in their own time, the battle lines would be faint and the comfort welcome.

When he lifted his head again, Matt told her, "Then, we'll stay here. Together. And make the most of whatever happens to us. I don't think the government's going to let that happen, though. There's more to this whole situation than a botched transportation."

"That's what I've been thinking, too," she admitted. "I mean, why me? Why was I chosen? There were two or three others in that room who *wanted* to take the A-train to Blitzville. All I wanted to do was expose Madame Olga as a fake."

Matt chuckled. "So much for that exposé."

"Not to mention the NYPD's case against her," Kate pointed out.

"Yeah, I can't wait to write up this report."

"You never did like paperwork."

"And you never liked being aced out of a scoop," he retaliated.

Their verbal bantering brought back warm, wonderful memories and she basked in their glow. "I didn't miss too many, thanks to you."

"Hey, Cricket, don't go accusing me of leaking valuable police information. I'd never—"

She laughed out loud, and recalled, "Our pillow talk usually consisted of who shot who, and who was under suspicion. It's a miracle we ever—"

Her thoughts caught up to her words and she stopped short, unable to finish the intimate recollection. "I mean—" Turning away, she blinked back unwanted tears, knowing exactly what would happen if Matt saw the damming evidence of her emotions.

"Listen, Kate," Matt said softly, "I'm going to get out of here for a little while. I want to check with Ezekiel and Esther and see if they've come up with any other information. Or, if we're lucky, a more fool-proof way home."

Kate nodded her head, but didn't answer.

"I'll be back in a bit."

The sound of the door closing behind Matt caused her stanched tears to fall in earnest. "Bye," she whispered, knowing he couldn't hear her. "Just like the old days," she choked back, emotion burning her throat, "run away like you always do when the situation gets a little sticky."

SEVEN

Moving swiftly down the corridor, Matt cursed himself with every name he could think of, and a few new ones he invented for the occasion.

Thoughtless bastard! How could you just leave her like that!

He'd spent the past two years analyzing his inability to deal with Kate's pain, not to mention his own. Now, when he'd been given chance to redeem himself, he couldn't do it. He couldn't offer Kate what she needed. A piece of himself.

He found Ezekiel right where he'd left him, hunched over the computer console, studying his data printout. Esther, usually a mainstay at her life-mate's side, was nowhere in sight.

"What's new?" Matt asked, leaning over Ezekiel's shoulder and scanning the data sheets. The printout might as well have been written in ancient Greek for all he could make of it. Numbers and letters ran together like a well-stirred bowl of alphabet soup. No semblance of order. No pattern.

"We have isolated the problem that kept you from transporting with Kate. Unfortunately, it is not something that can be readily fixed."

"So, we're still looking at being returned at separate times."

"Or," Ezekiel explained, "at least by different systems."

"Different systems?"

"One of you could be transported from here, using Ramses, and the other from the transport pod in the main computer room."

"You sound skeptical. Is there a problem with separate transportation?"

"I am not sure. We have never encountered a situation such as this before and, like the error that brought you both to us, we are only now beginning to understand where we went wrong."

"We?" Studying Ezekiel carefully, Matt asked, "You make it sound as if our transportation was something you planned."

"No, of course not. Other than responding to Madame Olga's psychic prowess, we try not to interfere with the time continuum."

"Why do I get the impression you're being less than truthful?"

Ezekiel gathered his papers from the top of the computer console and stuffed them into his pockets. "I am quite sure I do not know what you mean. Since you and Mrs. Kelly have arrived here, we have gone out of our way to answer your questions. We have offered you—"

"Okay," Matt interrupted, "I'm sorry. This whole time thing is getting to me. I guess I'm a little stressed out." Shaking his head, he amended, "No, make that a *lot* stressed out."

"Your level of conscious brain wave activity was rather high."

"Excuse me?"

"My printouts show that during our attempts to transport, the measurement devices nearly reached maximum capabilities on both you and Kate, indicating an enormous amount of pressure on both your physical and mental receptor terminals."

"Zeke, old buddy," Matt said, shaking his head and draping his arm over Ezekiel's shoulders, "you've got to learn to speak English."

"I am speaking English."

"Early twenty-first-century English."

****

Kate sat up in the bed, anxious for the opportunity to escape the confines of the sterile hospital-like environment. She didn't like hospitals, had never liked them. Especially since—

"Hello, Kate," Esther greeted, coming through the door with an armful of clothes. "I have brought you something to wear."

Kate recognized her slacks and undergarments, but the blouse looked new. She took the items from Esther's outstretched hands and laid them across the foot of the bed. "Thank you."

"We had to make you a new uniform, ah, blouse. Right?"

Smiling, Kate nodded, "Right. Blouse."

"The other had a hole in it."

She flinched, Esther's simple explanation reminded her not so simply of failed transportation and her wound. "I would like to leave, if I'm allowed."

"I have made arrangements for you to be taken back to the presidential residence."

"Couldn't we stay with you and Ezekiel? I mean, it's not that I'm not grateful for the president's hospitality, it's just that I—"

When her thoughts and words faltered, Esther explained, "It is not my decision where you and Matthew will stay. The president has decided that, while you are here, you must remain a guest of the government."

"But—"

"What Kate's trying to say, I believe, is that she prefers the separate sleeping arrangements available at your place."

Kate looked up suddenly, surprised to find Matt lounging against the wall just inside the door. His slow smile unhinged her composure even further and, rather than agree or disagree with his claim, she busied herself with gathering her clothes and scurrying into the nearby bathroom to change.

****

Kate stood at the picture window of the suite she would once again share with Matt, her gaze trained, but not focused, on the passing of the boats in the harbor. Behind her, she could hear someone setting the table for the evening meal. Matt and Ezekiel sat on the opposite side of the large outer room, their heads bent over Ezekiel's latest calculations. At any other time in her life, she would have been beside them, eager to take part in planning their return, anxious to know every minute detail of the next step in their adventure. But, not today, not now. For now, all she wanted was to get as far away as the three-room suite would allow. She wanted to hole up in her tiny bunk-like bed and sleep until the past two days were nothing more than an insidious nightmare. Or, better still, a distant memory.

"Excuse me, Mrs. Kelly?"

Stepping back from the window, Kate turned to face the young woman who had spoken her name. "Yes."

"My name is Birgit. I have been assigned to assist you and Mr. Kelly with anything you may need while you are here."

"Right now," Kate told her, "the only thing I need is rest. I'm going to go to bed early."

"But your evening supplement is nearly ready."

"I'm not hungry."

Birgit followed her into the sleeping quarters. "Perhaps you would like me to prepare you a soothing herbal soak."

"Herbal soak?"

"I believe it is what your civilization calls a *bath*."

"Yes," Kate agreed eagerly. "A bath sounds heavenly."

While she undressed and donned the robe set out for her, Birgit ran water in the large marble tub which sat in the middle of the bathing room. To the steamy water she added a handful of scented herbs. "Your soak is ready, Mrs. Kelly."

"Please, call me Kate. Mrs. Kelly is—" She hesitated, suddenly reluctant to admit she was no longer *Mrs.* Kelly. Instead, she finished with, "so formal."

"While you are soaking, I will procure you something to wear during replenishment time."

"Thank you." When Birgit left the room, Kate slipped out of the robe and into the tub. Steamy, scented water engulfed her. Reviving her, yet relaxing her at the same time. She felt the lethargy seeping into her body, drawing her deeper and deeper into its sleepy hold.

A sudden, and unwanted, memory sprang to mind: images of two nights before, and the effects of the drugged wine and subliminal video. Could the herbal bath produce the same results, she wondered? Was there something in the herbs that induced sleep as quickly and as completely as the wine had induced her uninhibited sensuality?

Kate sat up suddenly, unwilling to be held captive by another of the future's mysterious devices. She had to get out of the tub. She had to escape—

"Kate? Sweetheart?"

Matt's voice barely penetrated the haze surrounding her, filling her head with visions of clouds and the sound of gently flowing water. "Matt?"

"I'm right here, Cricket. I've got you."

She relaxed in the security of Matt's hold, the prickly feel of the hair on his arms rough against her bare skin. From somewhere deep inside her foggy brain, another memory stirred...

"Quit wiggling, Cricket, or I'm going to drop you."

"My big, strong hero drop me? Never happen." *Teasingly, she shifted herself in his arms, her bare breasts rubbing sensuously against his equally bare chest.*

"I'm warning you," he said in mock anger, "I'm going to—"

Laughing, Matt stumbled forward, tumbling them both to the big, silk-sheeted bed, taking the brunt of his weight on his arms. Hovering over her like a barely caged tiger. "Now, see what you've done, Cricket?"

"Yes," she whispered softly, "I can see very clearly what I've done."

Matt stretched himself out full length above her, lowering his large frame against her, covering her with his hard body. "Can you feel what you've done, Cricket?"

Her breath caught, the simple brush of his aroused body against hers stealing any and all ability to draw air—arousing her as quickly, as completely, as she aroused him.

"Yes," she told him boldly, wrapping her hand around the part of him that wanted her most, "I can definitely feel what I've done." Pressing quick, hot kisses to his shoulder, she asked, "What can I do to make amends?"

"I don't know, but, together, I'm sure we'll think of something."

Together. The concept seemed alien now. *Together* hadn't been in her emotional vocabulary for two years now. Raising her head from Matt's shoulder, she demanded, "Let me down, please. I can walk."

"Walk! Hell, Cricket, you were so sound asleep, you'd have probably drowned in that damned tub if I'd have been a minute later checking on you."

"Why?"

"Why, what?" he asked.

"Why did you come to check on me?"

"I don't know. I just had this sudden urge to see where you'd gone."

"I'd have been all right. Birgit would have come back with my gown in plenty of time."

"Birgit? Who's Birgit?"

"The woman. She ran the bath for me, and then went to get me something to sleep in. She said she'd be right back."

"Cric...Kate...you came in here alone. Over an hour ago."

"An hour ago? But that can't be, I mean—"

"Shh," Matt cajoled, drawing her more tightly to his chest. "Let me get you into bed. It's been a long day and, in your case, a rough one."

****

Turning back the covers of the first bunk, Matt set Kate down on the edge of the bed. As efficiently as his shaking hands would allow, he dried her flushed skin from head to toe. Then, he laid her back on the bed and pulled the top sheet up to her chin. He leaned forward and pressed his lips to her brow, inhaling deeply, expecting the scent that had always been uniquely Kate. Instead of the powder-soft tease he anticipated, his head filled with the pungent aroma of spices, somehow familiar, yet different. Not like anything he could readily name.

"Matt?"

The drowsy inflection of Kate's voice told him that she teetered on the threshold of sleep, her body and mind ready, but her stubborn subconscious unwilling to give up and rest.

"Yeah, Cricket, I'm right here."

"Hold me. Just for a minute or two."

He hesitated, uncertain of his ability to comfort without wanting more. Like an avalanche, memories of his previous failures as a husband came back to haunt him.

"Please," she whispered, her soft entreaty tugging on his heartstrings as only she could.

He stretched out at her side, carefully, purposefully, keeping the sheet between them. Drawing Kate into his arms, he held her tightly to his side, pillowing her head on his shoulder. "Sleep, sweetheart. Let yourself go. You'll be safe with me."

"Yes," she said groggily, "safe."

When he felt certain Kate had fallen soundly asleep, he eased himself from the bed. Standing at her side, he took one last look at his sleeping wife...ex-wife...and brushed a stray strand of hair from her forehead. Then, leaving her to sleep, he went back to the bathroom to have another look at the tub and the remnants of Kate's bathwater.

What he found surprised him. The tub had been emptied, anything out of the ordinary gone. Any evidence—

Evidence? Evidence of what? Nothing's wrong here. Kate fell asleep, that's all. She's tired, worn out. There's no reason to speculate about anything more sinister than the fact that she's not recovered from her recent ordeal.

But what about this woman Kate claims to have seen? What about the strange scents, and the empty tub?

Hell, Kelly, even in this time and place, you can't quit being a cop. For all you know about technology, the damned tub could be on a sensor. Or, the woman Kate claims to have met could have come in through the other doorway and emptied the water. You should be more worried about Kate, and less about finding evidence that doesn't exist. The problem is, you can't stay away from Kate, and you can't stay with her when she needs you. You're one pitiful excuse for a man. Aren't you?

How, Matt wondered, do you ignore a very demanding conscience? Especially when said conscious knew you so well and always seemed to be right.

Where Kate was concerned, there were no easy answers.

EIGHT

The sound of Matt fumbling his way around the bedroom in the dark woke Kate from a sound sleep. Lazily, she rolled over in the narrow bed, adjusting the lightweight sheet as she went. "Matt?" When no reply came to her summons, she said more loudly this time, "Matt. For heaven's sake, turn on a light before you stub your toe."

Her directive met with an obviously surprised and very drowsy, "Huh? What'd you say, Cricket?"

"Weren't you just rummaging around the room?" she asked, her pulse picking up speed in anticipation of his answer.

"No, sweetheart. I was sound asleep."

Heart racing, Kate drew a deep breath to calm herself. Then, raising herself to her elbow, she commanded, "Lights on!"

The overhead lights came on suddenly, illuminating the room in seconds.

Groaning, and forcing himself to a sitting position on the edge of the bunk, Matt asked, "What's the matter, Kate?"

"I could have sworn there was someone in the room. I thought it was you trying to find your way to bed in the dark."

"I've been in bed for hours. As a matter of fact, it's nearly morning. You must have been dreaming."

"No," she said firmly, resolutely. "I'm sure there was someone here."

Matt pushed the sheet aside and stood. The sight of his naked body drew her gaze like a magnet. She swallowed. Her heart ran a second race within her chest, the rhythm set by desire rather than fear.

Their gazes met and held and she knew a moment's relief that it was Matt's smoky gray eyes that held her attention rather than his well-sculpted body. Oblivious, she was sure, to the effect he had on her, Matt reached for a nearby robe and wrapped it around himself, covering his body and breaking the spell that held her captive.

Like the well-trained detective that he was, Matt quartered the room in seconds, inspecting each and every nook and cranny until he stood opposite the door leading to the sitting room. "Door open," he ordered. The door lifted on command and Matt slipped through the opening.

Kate breathed a sigh of relief and willed her pounding heart to slow.

Within minutes, Matt returned. "Nothing out there, Kate."

He repeated the thorough process of inspecting the bathroom and declared it empty as well. "See, Kate, you must have been dreaming."

"I guess you're right," she said, despite her gut reaction. "I'm sorry I woke you. Come back to bed."

Matt flashed her one of his unnerving thousand-watt grins. "With you?"

"I mean," she stammered, "*go* back to bed. By yourself."

Still smiling, Matt slipped out of the bathrobe and laid it on the foot of the bunk, his back to her; the sleek curve of his shoulders and indentation of trim waist led her gaze to places she didn't want it to go. He settled into his bunk and rolled to his side, covering his body and head with the sheet in the process.

"If you want to leave the light on, Cricket, it's okay with me."

Kate experienced a sudden flashback, a sense of *dejá vú*, Matt's words revived her memories and made her feel something she didn't want to feel. Feeling only made you want. Wanting something you could never have meant heartache and she had promised herself she'd never, *ever*, hurt like that again.

"Lights off," she ordered firmly, unwilling to succumb to her weakness. A weakness honed from recurring nightmares for months after she'd lost the baby. A weakness she had indulged in every day of her life since she and Matt had split. A weakness she'd not had to show these past few nights only because Matt slept close at hand.

****

Well, that went about as well as could be expected.

What'd you want her to do, invite you to sleep with her?

Yes.

Not in your wildest dreams, hotshot! Do you think she's gotten over her fear of the dark?

No.

Matt rolled over in the bunk, his gaze aimed at the door to the sitting room. It took a few minutes, but his vision adjusted to the darkened room and he could make out the distinct shape of a table and lamp just beside the door panel. What if Kate hadn't been dreaming? What if there really had been someone in the room? Who was it and, more importantly, what did he or she want?

Could there really be more to this supposed *glitch* in Kate's transportation than met the eye?

Now you're thinking like Kate.

There's nothing wrong with that. Kate's one of the most intelligent women I've ever known. If Kate questions something, it's usually for a good reason.

You think Ezekiel's hiding something, don't you?

Yes, I do. I can't put my finger on it, but something's rotten in Futureworld.

****

Kate woke first, slipping from beneath the sheets and wrapping herself in a waiting robe. The over-abundance of heavy material swallowed her up, falling to the floor and pooling at her feet. The wide neckline slid to one side, revealing more than enough bare shoulder. Gathering the loose fitting neckline in one hand, she lifted the sagging hem in the other and scurried off to the bathroom, intent on making herself decent before Matt woke up.

By the time Matt climbed out of bed, she was dressed and standing in front of the bathroom vanity brushing her teeth. As if there'd never been a two year break in their marriage, Matt took his place at her side and reached for one of the disposable brushes. "Pass the polishing cream," he said, nodding toward what she still thought of as toothpaste.

"Polishing cream?" Teasingly, she commented, "My, my, but haven't we adapted well to futuristic jargon."

Shrugging, Matt stuck the brush in his mouth and mumbled something that sounded suspiciously like, "When in Rome."

They completed their individual tasks in relative harmony, the rhythm they'd established during their marriage easily remembered. Matt brushed, while she flossed. Kate combed and pinned while Matt shaved, moving in sync with one another in an intimate, ritualistic way. Only once did their steps falter when they both went backward instead of forward, bumping into one another so solidly that she nearly lost her balance, remaining upright only by the grace of Matt's steadying hands.

"Whoa, sweetheart," Matt cautioned, flexing his big hands and tightening the hold he'd taken at her waist.

Through the thin silk of her blouse, she felt the

105

heat of Matt's touch. Lifting her arms, Kate braced herself by placing her hands flat against Matt's shoulders. Rather than push away, as she'd intended, she clenched her hands, digging her fingertips into Matt's bare flesh. Raising her head, she met his gaze.

His eyes widened, and he drew a deep, audible breath. His hands flexed a second time, cinching her waist like a belt.

She silently ordered her hands to relax, to release Matt from their grip. Yet, the order given, her hands only tightened more, her nails making indentations in Matt's skin.

His dark eyes lit with a fire she had nearly forgotten, and the breath he'd been holding came out in a rush. "Kate?"

She would probably never know who moved first, or who moved second, but before her addled brain could comprehend the possible repercussions, Matt's lips were on hers. Soft at first, the kiss quickly escalated into a warm melding of mouths, a dueling of tongues and tastes never completely forgotten.

Long accustomed to following Matt's skillful lead, Kate moved when he moved, breathed when he breathed. She willingly took all he offered. It wasn't until he went a step further, drawing her to him, pressing his arousal unashamedly against her thigh, that she regained a small portion of the sanity she'd so quickly lost.

Turning her head to the side, she unclenched her hands and, placing them flat against Matt's chest, pushed as hard as she could. Despite her best efforts, Matt relinquished very little ground. Pulling her back into his intimate hold, he kissed her again, reminding her, in no uncertain terms, of how easily he could seduce her. Under the spell of his artful kiss, he slipped his hand inside her blouse and beneath the thin satin of her bra.

It was then that Kate realized one very important thing. She didn't want him to stop. The thought frightened her and excited her in equal measure.

"Matt," she whispered, "please."

The sound of her voice, so soft and pleading, brought Matt to his senses. What the hell had he done? What was he trying to do?

That, you stupid bastard, seems quite apparent.

Kate's breast burned the palm of his hand. The tightly-drawn nipple pricked his skin like the point of a stickpin. Her lips, pressed tightly against his, were hot and sweet. Although he knew he had to stop, he couldn't resist one last taste, one last caress.

"Cricket." The very soft, very intimate use of her nickname drew predictable results and, when she gasped, he took the advantage he'd pressed, slipping his tongue between her lips to sweep the inner recesses of her mouth, stealing one more taste to store in his memory bank. On cue, his hand relaxed against her breast, his fingers parting only far enough to snag the nipple between his knuckles for one quick, passion-inducing pinch.

Kate gasped again and, never one to lose an opportunity, he stole another deep kiss. When Kate pushed closer, he kneaded her breast one last time before grudgingly withdrawing his hand from inside the silken folds of her bra.

Anticipating her embarrassment, and possibly her anger, Matt took hold of Kate's shoulders and spun her around until she faced away from him, giving them both time to recoup their equilibrium. Then, he wrapped his arms around her and held her tightly, innocently. Burying his face against her hair, he told her, "I'm sorry, Kate. I didn't mean for that to happen."

"It's okay. I mean, it wasn't all your fault. I should have stopped—"

"Yeah, I know. We both got a little carried away."

Kate reached up and pulled on his arms, extricating herself from his hold. "I'm going out to order morning supplement. Is there something special you'd like?"

Yes. You.

Rather than voice his desires, and grateful that she'd not gotten truly angry, he teased, "Morning supplement? Now who's talking like they belong in this crazy place?"

****

"Well, Ezekiel, what do you have to say for yourself?"

Ezekiel took a seat opposite the large desk, his hand-held DataStor resting lightly on his lap. Rohn Carpenter would not be easily swayed, so Ezekiel chose his words carefully. "Things did not go as we had planned, I will admit. Still, we should be able to complete our original objective."

"It is said that our plan will not work. That, no matter how careful we are to keep the terrorists from traveling back in time, someone will eventually slip through. The people who support Westmoreland and his government are far more able to sustain repeated attempts than we are solutions."

"Our elders know how important it is that we set this injustice right. For the sake of the world as we know it, not to mention the mistakes of our past that could have been avoided."

"Do you think they suspect something?"

"I am not sure. Mr. Kelly asked many questions about the inaccurate transportation."

"Does he know the attempt was sabotaged?"

"No. He believes we overestimated Ramses' power."

"When will the next attempt take place?"

"Westmoreland has asked that we return Mr. Kelly tomorrow morning and Mrs. Kelly the day after."

"Will they go alone?"

"Not by choice. We will have to convince them it is the only way."

"Let me consult with the others. If we have to, we will take transportation matters into our own hands."

"But we do not have the equipment."

Carpenter only glared at him, sending an unmistakable message in the dark menace of his eyes and making Ezekiel wonder if perhaps the alliance had become as dangerous as the government they fought so hard to overthrow.

"I will keep you posted as to Westmoreland's plans."

"Yes, Ezekiel, I expect that you will. While we are waiting for our illustrious leader to make a wise decision, perhaps you could come up with an alternative set of coordinates. Just in case."

"In case of what?" Ezekiel asked, although he wasn't certain he truly wanted to know.

Rohn Carpenter stood and nodded toward the doorway, indicating that their meeting had come to an end, adding at the last minute, "Just in case."

****

After having breakfast in their suite, both she and Matt asked for permission to review the historic database one more time. Although he appeared wary of their request, Daniel Westmoreland graciously acquiesced to their wishes, escorting them to the room they'd occupied two days earlier. After using his own thumbprint to gain access to the smaller of the two computers, he left them to review files from the early twenty-first century forward.

No sooner had young Westmoreland left the

room, when Kate turned to Matt and asked, "Are you sure this is going to work?"

"No," Matt admitted. "The method certainly works in our time. Keep your fingers crossed. Give me the tape, sweetheart."

She took a roll of clear tape from the pocket of her slacks and, after tearing off a small piece, handed it to Matt.

"Now for my pen-light. Okay," Matt explained as he worked, "first, we shine the light on the computer identification screen so we can clearly define the fingerprint. See," he said, pointing to the illuminated area, "right there. Now, we lay the tape down over the print, wait a few seconds, and then peel it away slowly so that we don't smear the lines."

"You should have been a crook," she teased.

"Yeah, right."

Crossing the room to the large mainframe computer, Matt held the taped fingerprint up to the identification pad. Carefully pressing the tape in place, he pushed a sequence of buttons just as Ezekiel had two days before. After a number of whirs and beeps, the monitor lit up, displaying the message, "Welcome, Daniel Westmoreland, how may Ramses help you?"

"Bingo!" Matt exclaimed excitedly, "we're in!"

"Now that you've accessed good-old Ramses here, exactly *what* are we looking for?"

"Political records mostly. I have the strangest hunch that Ezekiel's not exactly pleased to be working for Westmoreland."

"Who would be? The man's a consummate politico, all flash and no substance."

"You have to admit, though, the man's got good taste."

"You mean his wife, Arianna?" Just the thought that Matt found the obsequious Arianna Westmoreland attractive turned Kate's stomach.

"No, silly. She's nothing more than window dressing. I was talking about the way he looks at you. Given half a chance, he'd probably pull the same moves on you, Mrs. Westmoreland tried on me."

"And he'd get about as far," she confirmed, inordinately pleased by the relief she could see washing over Matt's handsome face. "So," she asked, "what, other than Westmoreland's lascivious tastes, makes you think he's dirty?"

Shrugging, Matt said simply, "He's a politician, isn't he?"

For nearly two hours they poured through the outcome of every election, both national and local, from the year 2016 up until present day. The only constant factor seemed to be the GOP. What was once known as the Republican and Democratic parties disappeared in 2030, replaced by two main groups called the Liberty Stance and the Alliance Party.

Apparently, the Liberty Stance had become the stronger of the two, because the Alliance Party, had not won an election in nearly thirty years.

"Here, look at this," Kate said.

"What?"

"I've been reviewing the society pages from around the time of each election."

"High society and politics go hand-in-hand," Matt said jokingly.

"*Yes*," she said firmly, stubbornly. "They do. Without the backing of the financial leaders, a lot of politicians wouldn't get past the primaries."

"I agree. What did you find?"

"It seems in 2045, a lawyer named Sean Kelly was seen in the company of a young debutante, Melanie Trump—"

"As in *the Donald*?" Matt quipped, interrupting.

"I don't know. Now, be quiet and listen. It says

here, Sean Kelly intended to run for the senate in the national election later that year and the gossips were speculating that his reason for dating the lovely Miss Trump were to solicit funds for his election campaign."

"Smart boy. He must be related to me."

Maybe, Kate thought, her pulse picking up speed. *Wasn't that the name we'd selected? Caryn for a girl...Sean for a boy. In a past we've not even lived yet, has another woman succeeded where I failed?*

"Anyway," she continued, intentionally pulling herself from her unwanted thoughts and fears, "the next column deals with the debutante again but this time, her date is Peter Westmoreland."

"Westmoreland? Oh, my," Matt said theatrically, "the plot thickens."

"If this Kelly character was such a hot political ticket, why'd she dump him for Westmoreland?"

"Fickle, would be my guess. Maybe Westmoreland had a bigger—"

"Matthew!"

"Bank balance, Cricket. Bank balance."

"Would you please get serious for a minute here? Check the senatorial records for the year 2045. Let's see what happened to your erstwhile namesake."

Matt entered the necessary command and pressed the *transmit* button. Within seconds, the requested records appeared on screen. Scanning the monitor, he confirmed, "There's no Sean Kelly listed. Maybe he didn't get good old Donald's backing and had to drop out."

"Check to see if there's a declared candidate listing for earlier in the year. Did he back out before or during the campaign?"

Matt called up the file. "Nothing. He must have changed his mind right after striking out with the woman and her family's money."

"Very funny. Let's see if we can access the files

of the Bar Association. See if this Kelly was really a lawyer."

"Yeah, but, with the know-how to be a good crook."

"What'd you find?" she asked.

"Nothing. No lawyer named Sean Kelly listed with the New York State Bar."

"What'd he do, fall of the face of the earth?"

"Maybe he was con artist, and he got nabbed."

"If that's the case, then he must not have been a very good crook," Kate pointed out. "And, obviously not related to you."

"Obviously."

The relief she felt was overwhelming.

NINE

Much to Kate's dismay, she once again found herself seated beside Peter Westmoreland at evening supplement.

Now who's sounding like they belong here? Matt's words and the teasing tone of his voice sifted softly, reassuringly, through her thoughts.

The pleasant memory of Matt's voice faded quickly when Westmoreland asked, "So, Kate Kelly, what did you discover at the databanks today?"

The brush of Westmoreland's leg against her own forced Kate to shift in her seat. Without begin obvious, she hoped, she scooted her chair sideways in an attempt to put an additional few inches between herself and the president.

"Nothing much," she responded belatedly and far more sharply than intended. The uncontrollable change in the tone of her voice drew Matt's frown.

"What Kate means, I'm sure," Matt inserted smoothly, "is that the information contained in the historical computers is, ah, well it's—"

Matt's molly-coddling of the president drew her ire. The weight of Westmoreland's hand against her knee, drove her past any thought of political correctness and prompted her to finish what Matt had begun. "Contrived rubbish." Kate's pronouncement, accompanied by a sudden rush to her feet, met with collective gasps from the guests seated at the table. "And, Mr. President, I'd appreciate it if you'd keep your hands to yourself."

Matt rose from his seat as well, rounding the table to stand protectively at her side. "What Kate means—"

"He knows darn well *what I mean*, about the data *and* his hand." Leveling what she hoped to be a quelling glare at the president, she continued, "The information available in those databanks has been put there for show, nothing more than polished prose to make the government look good."

"Mrs. Kelly, I am sure—" Arianna Westmoreland began.

"So am I," Kate interrupted. "*Very* sure."

"I will have you know, *Kate*, that the facts contained on those data tapes are accurate beyond reproach," Westmoreland defended. "Whether you choose to believe the information contained therein is up to you. Do not forget, it is only by my generosity that you are allowed to study those archives. No other visitor, whether from our time or another, has ever been allowed access."

"There have been others?" she asked. "Ezekiel told us we were the first to stay, and that the others were only short bursts of time continuum energy."

"You are a very quick study, Kate," Westmoreland conceded. "I must question what else my erstwhile assistant, Ezekiel, has told you. Perhaps his loyalty, not to mention his security clearance, should be monitored more closely."

Were it possible to recant her words, Kate would have gladly done so. The thought of putting Ezekiel in jeopardy had never occurred to her when she'd spoken. "Ezekiel," she began, hoping to set things right, "has only answered our numerous questions with guarded candor. It is my own curiosity you should monitor. I tend to get carried away sometimes."

"Amen," Matt said softly, yet she heard him, as did everyone else at the table. Much to her chagrin, the president laughed outright.

"I would imagine, Matthew, that you have had

your hands full with this woman. A position, I might add, that would not be totally without pleasure I am sure."

Kate had the most overwhelming urge to slap the president's face. Yet, rather than follow her instincts, she clasped her hands together to hold them at bay.

"If you'll excuse us," Matt said, taking her hand in his and pulling her away from the table, "I think it would be best if we have our meal in our suite."

Peter Westmoreland looked as if he intended to insist they stay, yet the first lady intervened with a gracious, "As you wish, Mr. Kelly. I will have your evening supplement delivered shortly."

****

"Well, Cricket, you certainly didn't hold back, did you?"

Matt's presence, so close in the mirror-lined elevator, unsettled Kate far more, and in an infinitely different way, than Westmoreland had done when he'd laid his hand on her knee. In an effort to capture control of her emotions, she stepped sideways, putting space between herself and Matt. "What did you expect me to do? The man was groping my knee."

Matt chuckled, the deep, throaty sound enclosing her heartstrings and drawing them taut.

"I meant your no-holds-barred comments on the historical data."

"Oh. That." Shrugging her shoulders, she admitted, "I hadn't intended to be quite so—"

"Blunt?"

"Yes, blunt. It's just that he made me angry."

Despite her retreat to the opposite wall of the elevator, Matt reached out and laid his hand on her shoulder, turning her to face him with the easy twist of his wrist. When he used the tips of his fingers to raise her chin, she felt a sudden and not totally unwelcome rush of desire.

"Your unabashed bluntness, Cricket, is one of your most endearing qualities. A quality, I might add, that I've both cursed and praised many times."

"You have?" The infinitesimal crack in her voice seemed loud even to her own ears. Yet, if Matt noticed, he gave no indication. Rather, he let his hand fall to his side, and stepped forward through the open elevator door.

Holding the door with one hand, he gallantly bowed and extended his other arm outward to usher her into the corridor. "Home, sweet home, *Mrs. Kelly.*"

She drew a deep breath to quell her pounding heart and lifted her chin, sweeping past Matt as regally as a monarch ascending her thrown. "Hopefully, not for long."

Their meal arrived mere minutes after they entered the suite. The service staff had no sooner left, when Matt announced, "We need a plan."

"A plan?"

"Yes. Just in case they want to send us home separately. Something tells me, that's what they're intending."

"We can't let them do that. I mean, what if something else goes wrong? What if it ends up being like Ezekiel suggested? What if you end up back home, and I don't?"

****

Matt wanted desperately to wipe the look of panic from Kate's beautiful face. He also wanted to kiss the down-turned corner of her mouth and replace her frown with a smile. He wanted...

It didn't matter what he wanted. Kate, as well as her beautiful face and kissable lips, were off limits. He couldn't take a chance with Kate's life, or his own, by allowing his emotions to interfere with common sense. He closed his eyes for a brief moment, intent on wiping away the image of Kate's lips and reigning in his wayward emotions. The tactic worked about as well, or as poorly, as the cold shower he'd taken after this morning's steamy kisses. The only way to keep Kate from his most intimate thoughts was through total abstinence and distance. Just as he had done for the past two years. Unfortunately, at the moment, distance wasn't possible. And, as for abstinence—

"Penny for your thoughts."

"What?"

"All right. You drive a hard bargain, Mr. Kelly. I'll give you a quarter, but you've got to tell everything."

"Take my word for it, Cricket, right now my thoughts aren't worth a plug nickel. At least not to anyone but me."

"What then," she asked, changing gears as swiftly as a bike racer, "will we do tonight? I mean, until it's time to go to sleep."

He grinned, or, more precisely, he attempted a leer, wagging his eyebrows for additional effect. "We could always borrow another video file from Mrs. Westmoreland's eclectic collection."

Kate rolled her eyes in an exaggerated show of disgust, then dabbed her mouth with a linen napkin and pushed her empty dinner plate aside. "I kind of thought we might start making some notes."

"Notes?"

"I thought, if we wrote everything down, and then hid the notes on our person, we could take some of this information with us and neither Westmoreland nor Ezekiel would be any the wiser."

"I'd thought of that, too. Yet, what's to say we'll believe what we're reading, or even remember to read it, when we get home."

"Home," Kate said, sighing deeply. "You don't know how good that sounds."

He hesitated for a split-second before reaching across the table and taking Kate's hand in his. Her fingers closed gently around his and, although he knew he shouldn't, he stroked her knuckles with his thumb. "Yes, I do, Kate. I know exactly how good it sounds. As a matter of fact, the only thing that would be better would be having someone to go home to."

Her fingers twitched, the friction created by the nearly imperceptible motion sending shivers through his hand and arm. A look of panic filled her eyes. Boldly, he met her gaze and slowly lifted her hand to his lips. Massaging her fingers open, he pressed his lips to the palm of her hand.

"Matt, I—" she began, her words stalling when he kissed her palm a second time, and then a third.

He would have gladly, albeit foolishly he supposed, gone for a fourth taste of Kate's soft skin except for the fact that she pulled her hand from his grasp and laid it against his cheek. Slowly, seductively, she stroked his chin with her thumb once, twice, before drawing back and hiding her hand beneath the table edge.

"Listen, Cricket, maybe you're right. With a little bit of planning, we could put together some good documentation."

"Yes, I suppose we could."

Her agreement, he thought, seemed hesitant. Or, as his, were her thoughts anywhere but on the collection of futuristic data. "I'll look for some paper and a pen. You browse around the suite and decide what we want to catalog."

"First off, I want a complete description of the clothes. No one, absolutely no one, would believe how fashion has regressed. No one I know would forsake their designer clothes for a simtaki."

Matt chuckled, reaching out but not quite touching Kate. Instead, he gestured with an effeminate swish of his hand, and reminded her, "You, my darling Kate, have never owned a designer outfit in your life."

"No, but I know a number of people who do."

"Could you imagine your *mother* in a simtaki?" he asked teasingly.

"Or your sister-in-law?"

Their joined laughter, he decided, had a familiar ring to it, a comfortable harmony. Too comfortable. "Let's get started, Kate."

"I think I'll change into the simtaki Esther gave me when we first arrived."

"Change? Why?"

"That way we can describe exactly how it looks and where everything goes."

"Good idea, Cricket. I'll catalog some of the furniture while you're changing."

****

Kate slipped out of her slacks and blouse and into the rough-hewn garment, wondering why anyone would go backward with technology rather than forward. Staring at herself in the full length mirror opposite the first bunk, she shifted from one foot to the other and tightened the belt of the simtaki. Still, the thing hung like a potato sack, no shape and definitely no sex appeal.

Sex appeal? You?

She mentally warned her conscious to keep quiet, yet her teasing inner voice refused to be silenced.

Short people aren't sexy, Kate. You know that. To be sexy, you need long legs, and big—

"Kate?" The sound of Matt's voice from the opposite side of the door came as a welcome intrusion. "Do you need any help in there?"

"No thanks. I'll be out in a minute."

Slipping into her sandals, she raised the hood of the simtaki and walked to the door leading to the outer room, sparing one last glance at her shrouded reflection.

Yoda.

She sighed deeply, then walked through the door, certain that if Matt made some snide remark, she'd punch his lights out.

****

Arianna Westmoreland rolled over, stretched like a cat waking from a long nap and pushed herself to a seated position on the edge of the bed. Fully spent, her guest rolled over and made a half-hearted effort at enclosing her in his arms and pulling her back to his side. Far too easily it seemed, she pushed his hand away and slid to the farthest edge, out of his reach. On the table beside the bed lay the remnants of the inducements she had used to prepare her partner for their sexual entertainment.

Unlike Matthew Kelly, the evening's conquest had been more than willing to partake in the pleasures of the flesh. Why, when offered a chance to bed the president's wife, would any man refuse?

She didn't like being refused.

What had happened to all the real men? Arianna wondered. Angered that there seemed to be no answer to her rhetorical question, she reached out and shook the man at her side, drawing him from his reviving rest. "Enough foreplay," she told him hotly. "It is time to discuss our plan."

He opened his eyes and stared up at her. This was what he'd been waiting for, the reason he'd first bedded Arianna Westmoreland. Although, not necessarily the reason he'd continued to appear almost nightly at her beck and call.

Their plan.

"It has to be soon," she explained. "Before my husband gives the order to return our visitors to their own time."

"Why? What do they have to do with our plan?"

"Nothing. At least not intentionally."

"Well, then..." he prompted, suddenly wary of what was to come.

"You have to promise me it will happen soon and exactly as I demand it."

He knew what she wanted. She wanted his instantaneous capitulation. His agreement to whatever plan she had brewing in her devious mind. "Okay," he agreed. "I promise. It will be tomorrow, or the next day."

"You can go now," she told him, dismissing him as if he were a servant rather than her lover. Yet, he knew better than to complain. When all was said and done, Arianna Westmoreland would hold the reins of power in her well-manicured fingertips.

He dressed without speaking, preferring instead to watch the play of calculated emotion cross Arianna's beautiful face. He'd nearly reached the door of her suite, when she told him, "One other thing, Rohn."

"Yes?"

"When it is all over, I want Matthew Kelly to be charged with my husband's assassination."

Rohn Carpenter left the government building by the side door. Dismissed by the First Lady, he made his way through the back hallways and basement storage rooms until he reached an open exit. A door left open by one of Arianna's silent, ever-vigil, servants.

He needed to contact Ezekiel. With Ezekiel's unwitting assistance, the plan could be put into motion. Contingent upon Mrs. Kelly's overzealous curiosity, and fueled by a few well-placed rumors, there should be no problem putting the blame for the president's demise on their time-traveling guests. Once the president was assassinated, there would be no need to affect the Alliance's plans for Mrs. Kelly's return.

In their own time, Matthew and Kate Kelly would become missing person statistics.

In this century, they would quickly prove to be the government's perfect excuse for swift and exact punishment.

Rohn regretted only one thing. With the plan complete, his visits to Arianna would become fewer and farther between. Establishment of a new leadership would take time and money. Both commodities came easier to the rich than to members of the Alliance. Who would be the next president? By law, until an election could be held, the formal title segued to the president's heir. *Daniel Westmoreland.*

It would be Arianna who held the power at that point; Arianna who controlled the destiny of Planet Earth in the palm of her hand. Such power would surely prove to be an omnipotent aphrodisiac. Who would Arianna turn to then?

Who would ultimately rule the world from beneath the silk sheets of Mrs. Westmoreland's bed?

TEN

Matt sucked in a breath and willed his heart to cease its pounding. Kate turned full circle in front of him, arms akimbo, her unbraided hair flying wildly around her flushed face. Even in the strange, monk-like garb of the current day, she was the most beautiful thing he'd ever seen. It took all the willpower Matt could muster to keep from openly voicing his strong desire. Unfortunately, while he could control his tongue, he couldn't control his body.

Matt silently cursed himself, and his unruly body, wishing both he and Kate back in time, back to where they were safe. If possible, back even further to when they were young and in love. Hindsight, he decided, is definitely a bitch.

"Well?" Kate prompted, drawing him from his darkly sensual thoughts and back to the job at hand.

"Well, what?" he responded a bit testily.

"What can we say about the haute couture of the day?"

"It looks more like something from the eighteenth century or before."

Kate lifted the simtaki's abundant skirt in her hands, and agreed. "The style definitely leaves a lot to be desired. In this outfit, even the most beautiful woman would have trouble attracting a man."

"Oh, I don't know," he teased, "it kinda grows on you after a while."

"Yeah, sure," Kate responded with total disbelief.

He wanted desperately to tell her that *what* she wore had nothing to do with the fact that she could turn him on full tilt with no more than her smile. "Your outfit is no worse than those gosh-awful overalls that the men of this era wear."

"At least they have easy access. One zip and you're out of them. This thing," Kate said, tugging on the front of the simtaki for emphasis, "is worse than a Chinese puzzle box."

He gave her a head-to-toe appraisal, wagging his eyebrows for effect. "I might just be willing to take a crack at solving the puzzle."

"Very funny." The tone of her voice held a hint of nervousness, he noted, its uneven meter at odds with her offhanded comment. When he didn't comment in return, she told him, "Let's get started."

Matt scribbled notes as Kate explained, "First, there's the pockets. They're deep and slanted. Esther says they're made that way to carry..."

Although he heard every word Kate uttered, his thoughts were on anything and everything but the design of the simtaki. As she spoke, Kate turned from side to side, the gentle brush of her hair against her shoulders drawing his gaze. When she bent forward and lifted the hem of the simtaki, he couldn't help but stare at the sleek length of her leg, the rounded curve of her calf. Her hair fell forward as she moved and, when she straightened, the strands fell across her shoulders and into the v-shaped neckline. Matt's fingers itched with the notion of brushing the strands of fiery red silk from her bare skin.

"Are you listening?" Kate asked. "You haven't written a thing since I started talking about the length of the simtaki."

"Sorry," Matt muttered. "What about the way the thing closes?"

"The closures are similar to the Velcro of our time except that they're soundless and the motion is smooth instead of sticky."

Kate turned around until she faced away from him. The simple movement of her body sent a hint of perfume through the air, enticing him...exciting him. Tapping her fingertip against one of the closures at the shoulder, she told him, "See for yourself."

Matt reached out and took hold of one of the tabs holding the neckline of the simtaki in place. "You just pull on them?" As he spoke, he tugged slightly, undoing the first closure and pulling her backward at the same time until he felt the back of her legs brush against his thighs.

"Yes," she answered softly, breathlessly.

Lifting her arms, she reached for the second closure and pulled it loose. The neckline of the simtaki fell open, yet the infuriating garment stayed firmly in place.

Slowly, she turned to face him, the smooth shift of her body bringing them toe-to-toe.

"The shoulder closures are the easy ones," she told him, her calm voice a study in composure. The hot flush of her cheeks contradicted her seeming tranquility.

"Would you like some help?"

She nodded, and his heart skipped a beat. Tentatively, he reached for one of the ties at the front of the simtaki, stopping just short of actually tugging on the thin strings.

"Kate?" Although he was certain she understood what he was asking, he waited for confirmation.

She sighed deeply, then took his hand in hers and pressed it to her breast.

"Matthew."

He loved it when she called him Matthew.

He pulled on the first string, but the blasted thing refused to budge. He tried again, yanking harder the second time. As if his frustration wasn't aggravating enough, Kate had the audacity to giggle.

Matt growled, and she laughed all the harder.

"Before I tear this potato sack apart with my bare hands, do you want to explain what I'm doing wrong?"

"Don't insult my potato sack," she teased. "It opens in the back. These front ties are used for sizing."

He slid his arms around her and reached for the first closure. With a firm tug, he pulled it apart, baring Kate's skin to the stroke of his fingertips.

She shivered.

The second closure gave way and he pressed his palm to her bare back.

"Matthew?" she whispered.

He could hear her hesitancy. "Yes, Kate?" The sudden realization that, at any moment, she might change her mind frightened him. Yet, he knew he would accept whatever she decided.

"Kiss me, please."

That was the last thing he'd expected, and the very thing he wanted.

He took great pleasure in kissing Kate. He always had and, with any luck at all, he always would. Gently, he pressed his lips to hers. Boldly, she raised herself onto her tiptoes and increased the pressure of the kiss. It took only a moment for the kiss to escalate, reminding him of why their lovemaking had always been special. Volatile. Often bordering on total incineration, it was anything and everything but simple. His hands trembling, he reached for the third of the closures, but his fingers slipped and the damned thing snapped back into place.

****

Kate threaded her fingers through Matt's hair and drew him close. The lingering taste of coffee flavored their kisses, and she let the distinct flavor coax her into repeating the tasting over and over again.

She thought about suggesting he slip the simtaki over her head and be done with it. Yet, there was definitely something to be said for prolonging the excitement. Especially when the prolonging went hand-in-hand with Matt's potent kisses.

"There," Matt announced, his fingers working diligently on the last of the closures, succeeding where he'd failed only moments before. "I think I've got it."

The back of the simtaki fell open and forward, pooling in the space between them, baring her to the waist.

"It would seem so."

Matt caressed her with his gaze alone, heating the surface of her skin with his eyes yet making her flesh goose bump with anticipation.

"I'd forgotten how absolutely perfect you are."

His words were a caress of another kind, and she reveled in the sincerity she could read in his expression.

"Far from per—" He cut her denial off with a kiss, the slow, languorous stroke of his tongue against hers stealing any thoughts she might have had about being less than perfect.

The weight of his hands against her breasts made her shiver. The gentle massage of his thumbs against her nipples caused her to squirm restlessly for more.

In a game she'd nearly forgotten, he raised his hands and held them tentatively above the surface of her body. Her skin tingled, brushed alternately by the cooler air and the heat that radiated from Matt's hovering hands. The sensation was nothing short of erotic.

Then, just when she thought she could stand no more of the sensual teasing, he lowered one hand to her bare breast. With his other hand, he tugged at what remained of the simtaki, slipping it past her hips until it fell in a heap on the floor.

"One of us," she whispered, "is grossly overdressed."

"Be patient, Kate. There's no hurry."

"But—"

Matt silenced her attempt at protest with a kiss and she quickly forgot whatever she'd been about to say, her thoughts sent helter-skelter by the heat of Matt's mouth against her own. The bold foray of his hands across her shoulders, her back, her hips and then beneath her panties made her tremble with anticipation. She clutched tightly at the front of Matt's shirt, gripping the soft cotton with every ounce of strength she possessed just to stay standing and not melt in a puddle at his feet. When he slipped one hand between her thighs, she gasped.

"Please, Matthew."

He chuckled. Pressing his lips to the sensitive spot just behind her ear, he whispered, "I intend to, Cricket. I intend to."

Slowly, Matt turned her around, pressing a kiss here and there, drawing her back against him until the undeniable heat of his arousal pressed firmly against her hip. Holding her to him with one arm anchored at her waist, he pressed warm kisses to her shoulders and the back of her neck. Between their bodies, she could feel the movement of his free hand as he worked on the buttons of his shirt. When he'd shrugged out of his shirt, she felt the brush of his chest hair against her shoulder blades, the gentle abrasion inciting riot within her.

Kate reached backward and caressed Matt's cheek with her palm, then slid her hand upward and ran her fingertips through his hair.

"Cricket, sweetheart. I'm not sure I've got the strength for this or the patience."

Even though he tried to hold her in place, she

managed to turn in his arms, pressing her breasts to his chest.

Smiling, she told him, "Then let me."

Kate trailed her fingernails from Matt's shoulders to his waist and back again. She brushed her knuckles against his collarbone and then laid her hand flat against his wildly beating heart. With her other hand, she reached for the waistband of his jeans. Once she'd freed the button from its hole, she tugged on the zipper and slid it slowly over his arousal.

"Careful," he growled.

"Hmm," she responded thoughtfully, running her fingertip over his impressive length. His body responded by throbbing noticeably beneath her touch.

Kate drew a deep breath and grasped the top of Matt's jeans in her hands. Then, kissing her way downward, she sank to her knees in front of him, pushing the denim material to his ankles. In less than a heartbeat, Matt had kicked out of his shoes and socks. She tugged the jeans over his feet and tossed them aside.

The sound of Matt's ragged breathing urged her on. When she straightened and pressed her cheek to the front of his cotton briefs, Matt inhaled sharply.

"Cricket," he whispered. Taking hold of her arms, Matt drew her to her feet and into his embrace. Sweeping her off her feet, he carried her across the room.

"Door open," they commanded in unison. The metal sentry slid upward, and Matt stepped across the threshold and into the bedroom.

Kate barely noticed when Matt divested her of her panties and himself of his briefs. The cool surface of the *mating bed*, as she had dubbed it, did little to relieve the frenetic pace of their foreplay.

"Whatever you want, Cricket," Matt promised.

She knew exactly what she wanted, what she'd missed. Yet, try as she might, she couldn't seem to voice her desires.

"Matt, I—" Her words stalled. "I don't know. I mean—"

Matt silenced her by pressing two fingers to her lips. Next to her ear, he whispered, "How about letting me choose?"

She nodded, her gaze meeting his, her breath catching when he lowered his head to nuzzle her breast. With his fingertips, he blazed a trail downward, mapping the route she was certain he would take. Memories came flooding back and, with them, her confidence and daring. She threaded the fingers of one hand through Matt's hair and cradled his head in her palm, holding him to her breast. With her other hand, she kneaded the muscles of Matt's shoulders and back, working her fingers hard against his firm flesh.

A simple tug of her hand shifted Matt from one breast to the other.

"Matthew."

He raised his head. Their gazes met briefly, knowingly, before he lowered his lips to the valley between her breasts, alternately kissing her and stroking her skin with the tip of his tongue.

Kate closed her eyes in heady anticipation. She flexed her hands and then sank the tips of her fingers into Matt's hair, urging him on, coaxing him downward until she felt the first brush of his lips against her belly, and then lower until he'd settled between her thighs. With a gentle nudge, her urged her legs apart and buried his face against her aching sex.

It didn't take long for her to climax. As a matter of fact, if anything, she felt more than a little embarrassed by the speed with which she'd responded. Matt, bless him, pretended not to notice but, rather, tenderly kissed the inside of each thigh and began again, slowly this time, allowing her to relax and recoup before sending her over the edge for a second and third orgasm. By the time he'd worked his way back up to her breast, she felt as if she were about to jump out of her skin.

Unable to keep still, Kate slid from beneath Matt and raised herself to her knees to hover above him. Willingly, he lay flat on his back and let her take the lead. At the first flick of her tongue against his chest, his body stiffened. The muscles in his chest bunched and rippled. Beneath a swirling curtain of chest hair, a flat nipple sprang urgently to life. She playfully ran her tongue from nipple to belly button and back again. Against her hip, Matt's erection throbbed.

Kate coaxed him onto his stomach. She ran her hands across his back and shoulders, massaging, caressing. She kissed one shoulder blade and then the other. She lightly scored his back with her fingernails and then bathed the indentations with her tongue. Beneath her, Matt squirmed. She kissed his hip, and then his buttock and he had to shift to make room for his growing arousal.

Her hand flat against the slippery silk sheets, she slid her fingers beneath Matt's body and stroked his hardened flesh. With little more than the nudge of her hand, she urged Matt onto his back. When she bent her head and took him into her mouth, he cried out.

She couldn't remember when she'd ever heard anything half as arousing as Matt's exclamation of pleasure.

****

Matt grasped the sheet in one fist, clutching it like a much-needed lifeline. In his opposite hand, he held Kate's head, his fingers intertwined in her wild red curls. He closed his eyes tightly and held his breath, certain that if he dared to breathe he'd lose the very last of his already tenuous control. Then, when he could stand it no longer, he tugged gently on Kate's hair and pulled her from her task, guiding her upward until their lips met.

"Kate, sweetheart," he mumbled against her lips.

He grasped her hips, stroking the soft but firm flesh with his hands, stealing a few seconds to recoup. She pressed her mouth to his, then slid her tongue across her lips, bathing them both in liquid fire. Matt ran his hands across Kate's thighs and encouraged her to straddle his hips and lower herself into place.

He bit his lip and prayed for control. He'd nearly forgotten how wonderful it felt to be buried inside Kate's body. Nearly, but not quite. She rocked forward and back, and he silently cursed and praised her innocent expertise. He sat up and drew her into his arms, wrapping her in a tight embrace, pressing her breasts to his chest. Legs and arms securely entwined, they took their time, stroking slowly, deeply. He cradled her head in his hands and drew her forward, gliding his tongue past her lips and teeth until he stroked her mouth in a perfectly duplicated rhythm.

Had it always been this wonderful? Had they always moved in such perfect harmony? He knew the answer as surely as he knew his own name. As surely as he knew that two years of being apart hadn't dulled the love he felt for Kate. As surely as he knew that he couldn't hold out much longer...

"Sorry, Cricket, I can't—"

Kate cried out, then pressed her mouth to his, stealing his apology and his breath with one deft sweep of her tongue. Pushing him backward, she sat up straight, taking him inside her until he could go no further. Within four, maybe five, frantic strokes she brought them both to a climax, collapsing on his chest when she'd finished, accepting his kiss and the gentle stroking of his hand against her hair as if there'd never been a two year hiatus in their lovemaking.

As if they were still happily married and safely at home...

ELEVEN

Esther ran her hand across the keyboard of Ramses' control panel, her eyes closed, her senses guiding her through the program. It had been a long time since she'd used her powers, a long time since she'd done anything so remotely dangerous. Yet, Ezekiel had asked. Despite her reservations, she knew she couldn't refuse him. Not even if it meant breaking a promise.

The palm of her hand itched and tiny frissons of warmth guided her from key to key. The sound of her rapid breathing filled the room, echoing around her, reminding her of the laws she'd had to break to gain access to this restricted area.

What secrets do you hold, Ramses? What part of your data has been compromised? Can you tell me who to trust? Of whom should we be wary?

She opened her eyes and stared at the monitor, the glow of the computer screen intensifying with her perusal. Lists of names scrolled across the screen, their progress halted by the press of her fingertips against the keys.

Membership to the Bar Association.

What possible use could there be for a listing of lawyers. Especially a list nearly twenty years old? Her fingers danced across the keypad.

Search. The cursor bleeped once, twice.

Kelly, Sean Patrick. DOB unknown. Records on file...none.

Again, Esther stroked the keys and waited. The screen changed, the files rolling forth one after the other, spewing out newspaper clips. Society articles.

Her hand, hovering scant millimeters from the surface of the keys, tingled and she extended her fingers to dispel the strange sensations.

A thought came to her. More important than which data had been accessed last would be the identity of the person doing the accessing. Quickly, smoothly, she changed course, slipping back into the guise of the system administrator. She typed in the necessary commands and waited for the requested information.

Daniel Westmoreland. What possible reason could Daniel have had for accessing information? Did the ambitious young man know more than he should? Did he have any idea *why* Ezekiel had aided in Kate Kelly's transportation through time?

More importantly, how had the government's top security forces missed erasing Sean Kelly's name from the society pages? What possible ramifications, if any, could this one loose piece of information cause?

The answers she sought were as rhetorical as her inner questions. What she needed were facts. Cold, hard facts.

Esther closed her eyes again, choosing to rely on her extra-sensory abilities rather than her knowledge of computer programming. Fact, both cold and hard, could be accessed at any time. Secrets, must be divined.

****

Kate rolled over in the big bed. The silk sheets rubbed softly, sensuously against her bare skin. She stretched out her hand and reached for Matt, even though her senses told her he'd already vacated his side of the bed.

She pushed her hair back off of her face, not the least bit surprised when her hand trembled slightly. Last night had been a mistake, albeit an enjoyable mistake. She'd spent the last two years doing her best to forget the wonderful sensations Matt's lovemaking had always inspired. Then, she'd spent the subsequent time since their divorce regretting that she and Matt could never talk in the way they should have talked, especially after the loss of the baby.

Their son. The one they'd intended to name Sean. Sean Patrick—

Sean Patrick Kelly!

Her pulse racing, she bolted from beneath the silken covers. Oblivious to her state of undress, she grabbed the robe that lay draped across a nearby chair, pulling it on as she made her way to the bedroom door.

"Door open!" With a sense of satisfaction, she realized even the most stubborn of futuristic apparatus could not ignore the strength of her command.

"Good morning, sleepyhead," Matt greeted. He hoisted a cup of coffee in salute then pressed the cup's rim to his smile. Before she could respond, he added, "I'll call downstairs and order your breakfast while you shower."

"There's no time for breakfast," she told him. "See if they'll let you contact Ezekiel." Half-way through the bathroom door, she stopped and turned back to add, "Make it sound like a social invitation."

Kate slid beneath the hot water and gratefully let its pulsating spray ease the slight ache from her body. The first glide of her hand across her breast made her wince. Whisker burn obviously didn't mix well with bath soap. As much as she'd like to relive the night before, if only in her thoughts, she had no intention of wasting precious time dawdling in the shower. Her questions required answers; her curiosity, appeasement.

It didn't surprise her to find Matt waiting just outside the shower door, his arms spread, a bath sheet stretched wide between his big and capable hands.

"Do you want to tell me what's got you in such a furor?"

She accepted the offered towel. The fact that Matt made no move to do anything other than wrap the huge towel around her shoulders gave her a moment's disappointment. Rather than give in to the emotion, she told him, "I don't know. Exactly."

"Give me a hint."

Although she would have preferred he leave the room while she dressed, Kate knew he would go nowhere until she answered. With as much aplomb as she could muster, she laid the bath sheet aside and reached for her bra and panties.

"I know this might sound crazy," she began, "but, what if our trip into time wasn't a fluke? I mean, who's to say there aren't other people out there zapping around the time continuum."

"What are you suggesting? That, maybe, we were brought here on purpose?"

She nodded, then contradicted herself by shaking her head in the negative. "Me, maybe, but not you. You were definitely a mistake."

"Thanks." The sarcastic bent to his voice drew her smile and his responding grin.

****

Was last night a mistake as well, Cricket? Matt couldn't keep the thought from sinking into his subconscious.

What'd you expect? Did you think she'd come looking for an early morning quickie? Silently, Matt cursed his inner voice, damning it to the far reaches of this strange place and time.

Oblivious to his inner dialogue, Kate explained, "Remember. You said yourself, something didn't seem right. You even suggested that maybe Ezekiel was hiding something from us. Something vital to our being returned to our own time."

"I think I'm going to need another shot of caffeine. Something tells me you've come up with another one of your bizzaro explanations."

"Bizzaro?" she repeated, laughing at his choice of words. "I'd prefer the term *creative*." Without letting him comment, she asked, "Were you able to get in touch with Ezekiel?"

"No, but the switchboard put me through to Esther. She's going to try and reach Ezekiel and have him come by."

Matt left her to complete the rest of her morning ritual in favor of pouring himself another cup of coffee. If Kate really did have another of her hunches, he knew he'd need his wits about him just to keep up. He'd need the extra boost of caffeine-driven adrenaline. If he'd learned only one thing in the time he'd known Kate, it would be the fact that her instincts, as bizarre as they sometimes seemed, were rarely off the mark. His heart raced just a touch faster, driven by an exciting combination of the coffee and the thought of, once again, watching Kate in action.

Ezekiel arrived within the hour and Matt welcomed him into the suite. "Thanks for coming right away."

"Is something wrong, Matthew?"

Ezekiel's concern seemed real, Matt noted, and he wondered if, perhaps, Kate might be wrong. Yet, as she'd pointed out, he'd also expressed some concerns about things not being *right*.

"Why don't you have a seat. I'll let Kate know you're here. She'll be able to explain better than me."

No sooner had he invoked her name when Kate came through the door, her arms laden down with the items they'd intended to catalog last night, right before they'd been so intriguingly sidetracked.

"Hello, Ezekiel," she greeted.

"Hello, Kate. What is it you wanted to ask?"

"Why did you bring me here?"

Confusion clouded Ezekiel's face and Matt felt a moment of pity for the man. Kate's question, straight forward as it was, clearly caught Ezekiel off guard.

"The president insisted," Ezekiel explained.

"No," Kate corrected. "I don't mean *here*. I mean to this time."

"I explained that to you already. Madame Olga..."

"Baloney!"

"Baloney?" Ezekiel repeated in question.

"Do you know what I think?"

If Matt had had a camera, he would have snapped a picture of Ezekiel at just that moment. In retrospect, Matt wondered how often in the past he'd worn the same befuddled expression himself and hadn't even realized it.

"I am sure, Kate Kelly," Ezekiel said slowly, deliberately, "that you are going to tell me *exactly what you think*."

It wasn't like Ezekiel to be so openly sarcastic. Yet, the inflection of his voice literally reeked with impatience and sarcasm. *Has Kate's curiosity upset you? Is she onto something you'd rather keep hidden?* Matt turned his attention to Kate, anxiously awaiting her response.

Rather than acknowledge Ezekiel's tone, Kate barreled ahead. "I think you had a purpose for bringing me forward in time and you used Madame Olga's abilities as a Medium to assist you. Matt's transportation may have been unintentional, but mine was not." When Ezekiel didn't respond, she asked, "Am I getting warm?"

"Getting warm?"

"Don't hedge with me, Ezekiel. You know exactly what I mean." Kate drew a breath and then continued. "There were six other people in that room, any one of which would have gladly taken a free ride into the future. Why me?"

"Perhaps because you were the most skeptical person at the table," Ezekiel suggested.

"Second most skeptical," Matt corrected. "Kate at least has a sense of adventure, while I have none."

"What possible reason could we have had for choosing you specifically, Kate?"

"Sean Patrick Kelly."

Ezekiel's jaw twitched, the slight movement barely discernable, yet Matt saw it, and he suspected Kate had as well.

"Who," Ezekiel asked calmly, "is Sean Patrick Kelly?"

A sudden rush of anger, hurt, settled in the middle of Matt's chest. "He would have been our son," he explained. "If he had lived."

"I do not understand."

"Okay. Let's say you don't know what I'm talking about," Kate conceded. "Maybe Madame Olga was assisting someone else to send me forward. Just tell me this, if you and Madame Olga can bring me forward in time, is it possible for someone from this time to go backward? Could someone go back, commit a crime, and then return to this point in time?"

"Anything is possible, Kate. After all, we did experience a glitch in Ramses' system that sent you back to 1880. However, that does not mean time travel is taken lightly, nor do we make it a habit to bounce back and forth between centuries. I believe you have watched too many science fiction films. I believe—"

"Oh, no," Kate interrupted. "Matt and I used to watch sci-fi all the time and, I can tell you, nothing we ever watched could hold a candle to the strange things we've seen and done since we've been here."

"If it will put your mind at ease, Kate, I will look into the possibility that others may be experimenting with time travel between our two time periods. I will put the word out within the academic community—"

"Will you contact someone within the Alliance? Will you ask if there are political factions interested in time travel experiments?"

Ezekiel raised himself from the chair and looked down at Kate. "I will do what I can. However, I am not sure there is anything to discover."

The moment the door closed behind Ezekiel, Matt turned to Kate in question. "Okay, Kate, tell me what's going on inside that beautiful head of yours."

He could almost see Kate's mental wheels turning. She hesitated for barely a heartbeat before she asked, "Did you see that twitch? He knows something he's not admitting to."

"I agree, Cricket. There's definitely more going on here than meets the eye."

His agreement only served to escalate Kate's excitement. "We may have been transported into the middle of some major political upheaval? Maybe even another war?" The more she hypothesized the more animated she became. "Look around, Matt, we're virtual prisoners of the government. Why all the secrecy? Why is everything, especially certain of the databanks, so off limits?"

Honed by years of practice, he deftly dodged the swinging of Kate's hands as she spread her arms wide to encompass their luxurious *prison*.

"Okay, Cricket," he interjected when she'd finally stopped to take a breath, "what's the bottom line? What do you suspect?"

"I think, no, I know, I was brought here for a reason. And, I suspect it has something to do with our baby."

The mention of their lost child brought tears to Kate's eyes, the sight of her quickly slipping composure bringing a lump to his throat as well.

"What if—" Kate began, only to stop when emotion constricted her ability to speak.

Matt reached out and took Kate's hand, drawing her from her chair and into his lap. Once there, he pressed her head to his shoulder and felt the first of her tears soak through the front of his shirt.

"What if," he said softly, "You let that over-active mind of yours rest for a little while?"

"But—" she tried again, yet the thickness of her voice told him she couldn't finish what she'd begun.

With the gentle touch of his hand, he lifted her chin and met her tear-filled gaze. As carefully as he could manage given the pounding of his heart, he kissed away the remnants of her tears and held her close. It took a moment for her to readily accept his offer of comfort but, when she did, when she relaxed back into his embrace, he released a deep sigh and relaxed a bit himself.

Giving comfort, he suddenly realized, could be as heady an emotion as love, yet infinitely less complicated.

TWELVE

Esther paced the width of the room once, twice and then a third time before she turned to her life mate and asked, "What do you intend to do?" Before Ezekiel could answer, she added, "How much do they know? How accurate were Kate's assumptions?"

Ezekiel shrugged, yet concern etched his usually composed features. "With Kate Kelly it is hard to tell how much she knows and how much she only suspects. However, given her intelligence, it will not take her long to deduce the entire story."

"*I* think you should tell them the truth."

"I cannot. The Alliance would not approve."

It wasn't often she felt the urge to argue a point with Ezekiel but, in this instance, she had no compunction whatsoever about voicing her opinion. "*The Alliance.* What have they done lately to deserve your loyalty, Ezekiel?" Folding her arms across her chest for emphasis, she told him, "Nothing! They let you face President Westmoreland alone. They allowed you and your family to accept blame for the failed transportation even though it was *their* idea."

"You do not understand—"

"What I understand is that the President, or at least his son, is onto us. They know we have a specific interest in Mrs. Kelly and that her transportation was *not* an unwelcome coincidence."

"And, exactly, how would they know that?"

"When I performed the review of Ramses' usage, I discovered an access of information code. The files accessed held clips of society columns which named Sean Kelly. An obvious oversight by the previous government's eradicators."

"A society column," Ezekiel repeated.

"That, and a listing of the New York Bar Association membership. According to the society column, Sean Patrick Kelly, Attorney-at-Law, was squiring around a young socialite. The next society column had that same woman dating Westmoreland. Following the review of the society columns, the next program accessed was the Bar records."

Ezekiel sighed deeply and closed his eyes.

Esther waited patiently for her life mate to gather his thoughts.

"Who did the accessing and when?"

"Daniel Westmoreland. Day before yesterday at 13:37."

Ezekiel shook his head. "That is not possible. Daniel was with me. We were comparing our notes on the return projections."

Esther reached into her pocket and withdrew the neatly folded printout. "Here," she told him, "see for yourself."

Ezekiel stared at the piece of paper and, after a moment's hesitation, took it from her hand and read it. "This is not possible."

"The computer confirms entry by a fingerprint scan."

"So it would seem." Again, Ezekiel assessed the printout. "But how is that possible when Daniel was with me?"

"I do not know."

She could almost see the wheels of Ezekiel's analytical mind turning. His eyes lit with an excitement she had not witnessed in a long time.

"What is it?" she asked when her curiosity could no longer be contained.

"You are the computer expert, Esther. Is it possible Kate or Matt could have somehow duplicated Daniel's print and used it as their own?"

"Not that I know of, yet, if we have discovered nothing else, we do know they are resourceful and daring."

"Perhaps they know of some way to duplicate fingerprints. History records many forms of trickery in the pursuit of ill-gotten fortunes. Perhaps, as an officer of the law, Matt would know these things."

She nodded in agreement. "With these two, I would imagine anything would be possible. That is why I believe it would be in our best interest to talk to them. They did not ask to be brought here and they deserve to be told the truth."

Ezekiel reached out and laid his hand against her cheek. "Why is it," he asked, "that you always compel me to do what is right?"

As always, she felt the magnitude of Ezekiel's love in the warmth of his touch. "That is simple, *husband*, you are a good man and you know an intelligent woman when you see one."

****

Curled up in the largest of the suite's chairs, Kate held pen and paper in hand. "Okay, Matt, let's go over this again."

He poured himself a cup of coffee and took the seat directly across from Kate's. "What's first on the list?"

"First off, we have the existence of Sean Patrick Kelly, albeit a very poorly documented existence."

The last few words seemed to stick in her throat and it was all he could do to keep from pulling her into his arms and offering comfort. Wanting to alleviate her obvious anxiety, he said simply, "And we have a well-situated socialite."

"Yes. We have references to Sean Kelly being an attorney, yet, no Bar Association listing." Tapping the tip of the pencil against the pad of paper, she wondered aloud, "Do you think it is possible that Sean Kelly was licensed in another state?"

"Possible," he agreed. "That might explain his sudden disappearance from the public eye. Suppose he and the lovely socialite had a falling out over family money and he packed his bags and went home to—"

"That's just it, to where? If New York, excuse me, Ankara is all there is left of the civilized world, where else could he be from but here?"

"Don't forget, those society pages were from years past. How long has it been since there were no other big cities or Bar Associations?"

"We need another shot at the computer," Kate stated firmly. "As Daniel Westmoreland, of course."

"I don't know, Cricket, things are getting tight around here. The chances of our being given a look at the accessible databanks are probably slim to none, never mind the possibility of obtaining another print."

"We can at least ask. What harm can that do?"

****

Less than an hour later, they were ushered into the data storage area. Unfortunately, it was Arianna who escorted them rather than Daniel. Kate couldn't help but feel a bit apprehensive about the ease with which their request had been granted.

"What is it you want to find?" Arianna asked.

"Nothing in particular," Matt told her, "we were getting a bit bored sitting around the suite and thought we might surf the net for entertainment."

"Surf the net?" Arianna repeated in question. Leaning a bit too close to Matt for Kate's comfort, Arianna confessed, "I do not understand this term."

Matt smiled and explained, "It's a late twentieth-century term for accessing world-wide information via the computer."

"Oh."

"We don't want to keep you from your official duties," Kate suggested in hopes of getting Arianna to leave them alone.

She felt her stomach roil at the thought of having to cajole the other woman. Yet, Arianna had been the only access available, and a means to an end.

"There is nothing pressing," Arianna responded, "I have no need to rush away."

Resigned to Mrs. Westmoreland's company, Kate took her place at one console while Matt sat down at the larger mainframe. Using the steps Ezekiel had shown them on their first trip to the banks, she slipped into the computer's memory in search of a confirmation of dates and general background information. Hopefully, she would also be able to re-call more of the society columns she'd barely glossed over before. If information existed in one area, on one database, who was to say it could not exist elsewhere.

Matt, in keeping with their plan, would review sports columns and entertainment pieces. Much to Kate's chagrin, he would also distract Mrs. Westmoreland when necessary. Sometimes she hated her own schemes, even when they netted results.

****

"So, how do I access the educational facility records?" Matt asked, drawing a far-too-willing Arianna back to his side.

Arianna leaned closer to where Matt sat and he was immediately overwhelmed by the aroma of her perfume. The difference in what women considered enticing from one century to the next was anything but subtle.

"Why do you want to access the academy records?" Arianna asked.

"I'd be interested in seeing whether or not they still have football teams and, if so, what the competition is like."

"Football? You are searching databanks for football records?"

He could almost hear Kate snickering. Far be it from him to spoil her fun. Hopefully, in the end, his diversionary tactics would prove worthwhile. He supposed he could make some pithy comment to her later about *feeling used* yet, most likely, to do so would only fuel her outright laughter.

Despite his misgivings about acting as a decoy, he had his hands full keeping Arianna on his side of the room. Almost as if she could sense Kate was up to no good, the First Lady kept glancing in Kate's direction. Lost in her perusal of the computer screen, Matt was certain Kate never noticed the other woman's curiosity. The thought that Kate trusted him to do his job, however distasteful it might be, made his heart swell with love. It made him feel—

"Hello, Matthew." The sound of Ezekiel's voice quickly penetrated Matt's consciousness, drawing his gaze to the doorway where Ezekiel stood, Esther at his side.

"Hello, Mrs. Westmoreland," Esther greeted. "I do not believe I have ever seen you here in the data storage area."

"I am doing a favor for the president. Both he and Daniel are otherwise occupied and Mr. and Mrs. Kelly had a sudden urge to entertain themselves with old football records."

Ezekiel did not comment, but a smile tugged at the corner of his mouth. Esther also seemed to be fighting amusement, almost forcing complacency. Their nearly duplicate reactions raised Matt's pique and made him wonder what had actually brought them to the data area. Did Ezekiel have answers to Kate's questions? Surely Ezekiel would not share his news in front of the First Lady.

"What brings you here, Ezekiel?" he asked.

"I have come with good news of sorts."

"Of sorts," Kate repeated.

Matt glanced at the computer console where Kate had worked only moments earlier. It did not surprise him to find that she had exited the system. While Arianna Westmoreland might overlook their browsing out of indifference or, as they'd found out, be easily distracted, it would be foolish to think Ezekiel would not be curious. Until they received answers to their questions, neither he nor Kate would willingly give any more than they got.

"We have established reliable return coordinates for your journey back to your own time. There is only one obstacle."

"Which is?" Matt questioned.

"The president is insisting transportation be done separately with a two day delay in between."

"No," Matt said firmly, resolutely. "It's together, or not at all."

"According to the president's advisors it is impossible to guarantee—"

"I don't understand the difficulty." Kate admitted. "You brought us here together. Why can't we go back that way?"

"We did not bring you here exactly. Madame Olga *sent* you here. We only aided her transmission. Now, Madame Olga is out of the equation so we must rely on Ramses for accurate transportation. Our earlier attempt proved Ramses can handle only one stress load at a time."

"But why the extra day delay?" Matt asked.

"To recalculate the coordinates," Esther explained.

Kate inched closer to his side and asked, "How will that affect us back in our time?"

"Hopefully, there will be no problem. At the time of transport, we will send Kate first and to an exact day and time. Then, when we send you, Matt, we will send you to the same day and time but a different location."

Matt glanced from Ezekiel to Esther, his gaze landing on Kate's pensive expression. "And that should work?"

"It is the best we can do. Daniel and I have worked separately on these computer programs and have come up with almost identical results. I did my best to convince both Daniel and the president we could affect dual transportation. However, the president expects..."

Despite the calm, assuring tone of Ezekiel's voice, Matt could feel his impatience rising quickly. Something needed to be done to impress upon these people that failure was not acceptable. And, instead of working on separate programs and then comparing results, it might be more advisable to work together for the good of the outcome. Staying here and never returning to their time and place would be preferable to being separated from Kate for eternity. Obviously, it would be up to him to bring those points to the attention of the man ultimately responsible for making the decision. Crossing to the doorway, Matt stopped and turned to face Arianna Westmoreland, "If you'll excuse me, Mrs. Westmoreland, I am going to go downstairs and speak to your husband. I don't believe he understands the concept of teamwork."

"Teamwork," Arianna repeated.

"Yeah," Matt told her sourly, "it's a *football* thing."

He had no idea whether or not he'd be granted admittance into the president's office. All he knew was he had to try. Rather surprisingly, passing through the corridors from one floor to the other had been no problem. The uneasiness he could feel creeping into his gut barely slowed him down. At the gateway to the world's most influential location, the reception desk stood empty. The sound of voices,

151

vague and coming at him from a distance he judged to be three or four offices away, caused him a moment's pause.

How different the situation from what he knew. If he were to attempt such a visit in his own time, he would have been accosted at the front door and ushered, rather unceremoniously, to a Secret Service holding area. Yet here, where building security relied on high tech scanning techniques, he'd gained unhindered entrance to the outer offices of the presidential suite and now stood on the threshold of the inner sanctum.

Tentatively, Matt knocked, and received no answer. No wonder security was lax. There was nobody home.

Forget it. Go back to data storage, get Kate, and talk things out with her. Together, you can decide whether or not to accept the president's decree.

Rather than listen to the urging of his common sense, he faced the doorway and said firmly, "Door open."

A computer-generated sentry announced, "Identification is required. Place your hand on the scanning pad to your right."

As requested, Matt placed his hand firmly against the brightly lit pad. The scanning mechanism rolled up and down the screen. Beneath the light, his palm tingled.

He shifted from one foot to the other, waiting for what he was certain would be a refusal for admittance.

"Welcome to the presidential offices, Matthew Kelly," the voice greeted. The door slid upward and Matt hesitated.

Something's not right, his sixth sense told him.

Don't be ridiculous, he argued back. *I only intend to talk to the man.*

Ignoring the warning of his detective's well-honed instincts and intent on making his point with the president, Matt walked through the open doorway and to the middle of the huge office. The room was surprisingly dim, the only illumination a lamp on the corner of the desk. He turned toward the light and started forward only to be stopped dead in his tracks by what he saw.

There, slumped over his desk and lying in a pool of blood was Peter Westmoreland, President of the United States and leader of Planet Earth.

THIRTEEN

"Son of a—"

Matt reached out and laid his fingertips against the pulse point on Westmoreland's neck. Nothing.

What'd you expect, detective? The man's dead!

Judging by the fact that the half dozen or so visible bullet holes still oozed blood, he guessed Westmoreland had been dead less than half an hour. Forty-five minutes tops.

Matt leaned closer, pulling the desk lamp with him and shining the light on Westmoreland's body. His eyes were wide open, his mouth contorted by a mixture of what Matt sensed to be both pain and surprise. Twelve years as a cop in Manhattan had given him the opportunity to see more than enough dead bodies and to develop more than enough theories on events that might have transpired just before a victim's death. Based on what he knew and what he could only hypothesize, Matt's first instinct was that the president knew his assailant. Knew and never suspected the person facing him would want to cause him harm.

He inspected the entrance wound in Westmoreland's cheek, the bullet's exit at the base of the president's skull. The second wound was one to the throat. At least four other holes were visible in Westmoreland's chest. The blood from the chest wounds painted a macabre picture on the president's starched white shirt.

Something about the wounds looked familiar. In a world that claimed no need for weapons or tolerance for violent crimes, suspicious. If he didn't know better, he would have sworn the wounds were made by a 9mm Beretta. Yet, that was impossible. There were no Berettas in 2065. Other than—

"Damn!"

He made a cursory search of the floor around the desk and along the window ledge, just in case the killer might have planted the gun in an obvious place never expecting him to come to the president's office.

On the other hand, what if Ezekiel's pronouncement of Westmoreland's decision about their return plans was intended to anger him and draw him to the president's office?

Face it, Kelly, you've been set up. Royally.

Had Ezekiel been the one to set him up? Or, as he hoped was true, had Ezekiel also been a pawn in a bigger scheme?

Matt assessed the most obvious exit route. Rather than go back the way he came, he crossed the room and stood in front of another doorway. "Door open," he ordered. Not surprisingly, the door didn't budge.

He could hear voices, their words muffled by distance but growing more distinct with each passing second. It would be only a matter of time before they reached the office door. He moved along the back wall, being careful to avoid the picture window that filled one side of the room. In the right-hand corner of the room was another door and Matt ordered, "Door open."

The metal sentry stayed firmly grounded to the floor. The voices grew closer, the very prominent meter of Daniel Westmoreland's speech the first one he recognized. Pressed to the third wall, Matt hovered in the shadows and felt his way along the book-lined shelves. He stopped suddenly and turned to face the wall, his gaze assessing the shelves from floor to ceiling in one efficient sweep.

Forget it! There's no way in hell.

He pressed his hands to the wall and slid them along the seam of each wooden panel. While he didn't hold much hope of finding a *secret passage*, the idea of there being a bolt hole in the executive office wasn't totally out of the question. From behind him, he could hear the conversation between Daniel and—

"I'm telling you, Daniel," Ezekiel said firmly. "You're calculations are incorrect. My last set of numbers proves that a dual transportation is possible."

"Well, then," Daniel responded somewhat defiantly, "we will have to tell my father. If Mr. Kelly is still here, you can give him the good news as well."

"I am sure Matthew will be most pleased," Ezekiel began, only to end with, "Oh, my! What has happened here?"

At the same moment, Daniel cried out, "Mr. President! Father!"

Matt leaned back against the cool brick wall inside the hidden passageway and sighed. That had been too close for comfort.

You're one lucky son-of-a—

He cut his internal voice off at the pass, shaking his head and bringing himself back to the matter at hand. Considering the passageway existed, it would be entirely conceivable Daniel could know of it. He didn't dare risk waiting around to find out.

****

Kate paced the sitting room of their suite, wondering what had become of Matt and anxiously awaiting his return. Had her quick-to-anger ex-husband given Ezekiel a chance to explain, Matt would have found out about Ezekiel's theory for a dual return. But no, not Matt. The minute things didn't go as he wanted; the minute there were two defined sides, the bad guy and the underdog, Detective Matthew Kelly felt compelled to intervene. Stand up for the little guy; keep the city safe.

Leave your wife waiting while you play hero.

She shook her head, dislodging the memories. With a brush of her fingertips, she wiped away the one tear that had dared to escape. About to begin another circle of the large room, she stopped suddenly when the door to the suite slid upward. Blinking her eyes to dispel any lasting tears and to set her *I'm-just-as-strong-as-you-are* mask in place, she turned to greet Matt.

Instead, she came face-to-face with two very large men. On their bent arms rested what appeared to be some sort of futuristic weapon. A cross between a machine gun and television satellite dish, the things looked both cumbersome and menacing.

"Is your husband here?" the first man asked.

"No, he hasn't returned from his meeting with President Westmoreland," she told them.

The second man took hold of her arm and drew her forward. "Are you sure?"

She twisted in the man's grasp, pulling free of his hold more by surprise than by any innate strength on her part. Before she could take a step in retreat, he'd captured her arm again and held on so tightly that she thought he might actually break a bone.

"Stop that! You're hurting me!"

The man only growled in return and pulled her to the door. The other man made a quick sweep of the adjoining rooms, confirming for himself that Matt was nowhere within the suite.

"I demand to know what's going on." She would have made a second attempt at escaping the man's grasp had he not tightened his hold even more when she spoke.

"You will find out soon enough, Mrs. Kelly. In

the meantime, we have been instructed to take you to the fourth floor detention area."

"Detention area?"

"Yes. You will be held there until your husband is found and executed."

"Executed?" She couldn't squelch the panic in her voice. What the devil was going on? More importantly, what had happened to Matt?

Daniel Westmoreland, Ezekiel, Arianna and Esther were waiting when Kate arrived at the detention area.

"Ezekiel? Esther? What is happening?" Kate asked.

Daniel stepped forward. "I will tell you what has happened."

Kate detected the slightest waiver in Daniel's attempt at anger and, without knowing why, she felt a moment of compassion for the usually insufferable child. "Okay, Daniel, explain."

"Your husband has assassinated the president."

Nothing Daniel could have said would have shocked her more. Her heart pounding, she turned from Daniel to where Ezekiel and Esther stood. Shaking her head, she muttered beneath her breath. "No, that's not possible." Tears welled up in her eyes and she did nothing to staunch their fall. "Matt wouldn't do that. Matt's a cop. He saves lives. He fights for the under..." Her words trailed off, lost in one long sob.

Esther immediately came to Kate's side, enveloping her in a comforting embrace. "I am sorry, Kate Kelly, but the evidence points directly to Matthew. It was his gun. It was his—"

"Then it can't be," Kate argued between gulps of air and the choking tears she couldn't stop. "He didn't have his gun. He gave it to the, to the—" Pausing, she drew another breath and said, "Esther, you remember. President Westmoreland took the gun from Matthew the very first time we met. He said guns weren't allowed and that Matt could have it back just before we were sent home."

"Yes, Kate," Esther said consolingly, "I remember. However, is it not possible Matthew could have retrieved his gun from the president's desk?"

Kate shook her head. "No, not Matt."

Arianna came forward and placed her hand on Kate's shoulder. Their gazes met and Kate felt a shiver work its way down her spine. Something in Arianna's eyes made her wary.

"Kate, I know you do not want to believe this has happened. I, too, find it hard to fathom Matthew could do such a heinous thing. Unfortunately, all the evidence points in his direction. And, according to our initial reports, Matthew was overheard arguing with Peter not ten minutes before his body was discovered."

Once again, Kate felt a tremor shake her body. Yet, it wasn't fear that drove the tremor but disgust. Arianna Westmoreland, she realized, showed no signs of being a grieving widow. No signs of remorse. Everything about her, from her stiff stance to her icy gaze spoke of cold calculation; the type of cold calculation necessary to commit a murder. Yet, up until half an hour before the guards came to haul her away, Kate had been in the computer room, and, so had Arianna.

"What was the time of death?" she asked, mustering up her strongest voice and reporter-honed skills of inquiry.

"Excuse me?" Arianna asked.

"The time of death. When do your people believe the president died?"

When Arianna only stared at her in confusion, she turned to Ezekiel and asked, "Surely you understand what I mean by time of death?"

"Daniel and I found the president nearly an hour ago when we went to tell him of my theories on dual transportation. When we arrived in the president's office, he was already dead."

Kate glanced at her watch, did a mental count back of the time and immediately eliminated both Arianna and Esther from the list of suspects. That left almost everyone else, but not Matt. "What will happen now?" she asked.

Rather too obligingly for her peace of mind, Daniel explained, "Security is out in full force. All exits have been sealed off and the streets surrounding the government buildings have been barricaded. It is only a matter of time before we find your husband."

"And when you do?"

"He will be executed."

Daniel's simple, non-emotional, answer caused her pulse to race and her heart to pound. Immediately, she felt a second rush of tears fill her eyes. Yet, the tougher, more resilient, Kate refused to let them fall. Summoning all the strength she could, she turned to face Arianna Westmoreland and stated firmly, "You know as well as I do, Matt did not kill your husband. He is being set up. And, if it's the last thing I do, I will prove his innocence."

Kate walked purposefully to the door, amazed at how steady she felt on the outside when her insides were threatening collapse. Only when she reached the door did it occur to her that she might not be let out of the room. Turning to face the others, she told them, "If I am not under arrest, I'd like to go back to my room." Her gaze swept the detention area and its inhabitants, as she added, "I have no desire to be here with *any* of you."

****

Kate lay curled up on the oversized chair in the sitting room of the suite thinking of Matt.

Remembering. Wondering if he was safe. What if they'd already found him? What if they didn't bother telling her and had judged him guilty without benefit of trial and then executed him on the spot? A tremor shook her entire body, and she clutched her chest where it ached. She couldn't bear the thought of losing Matt, not to death. Even if they never, ever were together again as man and wife, she couldn't survive knowing she would never be able to see him, hear his voice or touch him again.

She had about decided to go to bed when the door slid upward to admit one of the servants with a tray of food. Late night supplement. Through the open doorway, she could see at least two armed guards. Where they there to keep her in or to keep Matt out?

She spared only a fleeting glance for the tray of food, certain if she tried to eat anything she'd only lose it moments later. She was about to send the girl and the tray away when she noticed a piece of paper peeking out from beneath the largest plate.

"Thank you. Please leave the tray. Someone can come back in the morning for the dishes."

The girl nodded and exited through the still-open door. Kate waited for what seemed like an eternity until the door slid back into place. Plucking the note from beneath the plate, she unfolded it and read: *Don't even think about not eating, Cricket. You know how cross you get on an empty stomach. Besides, I'm going to need you strong and at your most intelligent to help me sort this out. Matt. P.S. I didn't do it! P.S.S. Don't come looking for me, I'm not in the building. I mean it!*

The weight previously crushing her chest eased somewhat and she felt the overwhelming urge to shout for joy. Matt was alive and relatively safe. And, in need of her help. A thousand thoughts ran helter-skelter through her mind. Where was he?

How'd he get the note to her? Who could she trust? Did the young girl know she was aiding and abetting? Hell, did she even know what aiding and abetting was?

Stop it! Get hold of yourself. If you're going to help Matt, then you need to start thinking logically. You need a plan.

****

"Are you sure Kate got the note?" Matt asked.

"Yes," Ezekiel assured him, "my niece took it to Kate herself." Almost hesitantly, Ezekiel asked, "What do you think Kate will do?"

Matt chuckled. "Knowing Kate, first she'll curse me out roundly for making her worry. Then, she'll start formulating a plan."

"A plan?"

"Don't look so worried, Ezekiel. Kate's plans rarely fail. Well, almost rarely."

Ezekiel shook his head. "Something tells me, Matthew, those of us on the outside are the safest."

He wanted to laugh, to revel in Ezekiel's understanding of Kate's little idiosyncrasies. Yet, the time had come for seriousness. Kate couldn't be the only one with a plan. Somehow, he and Kate had to find a way to communicate, to work together to solve Westmoreland's murder, because, until they did, they would never be able to go home.

"I'm grateful your friends found me," Matt said sincerely. "I must admit, I thought for sure I'd been discovered by the government's patrol. Had the men not mentioned your name, I'd probably have fought for my freedom."

"You were very clever, Matthew, to discover the alternate exit from the president's office. I am certain there are very few people who know of its existence."

About to comment, he stopped short when he realized Ezekiel was staring past him. Matt turned to see another man coming up behind them. "You never did explain how you discovered the passage, Mr. Kelly." The man's deep, serious tone put Matt on alert.

Ezekiel stood and greeted the tall man with a handshake. Nodding toward where Matt sat, Ezekiel said, "Matthew, this is Rohn Carpenter. Rohn is the leader of the Alliance. It was he who ordered our men to go in search of you and bring you here."

Matt stood and extended his hand to Carpenter. "Thank you. I'm not sure I would have been able to elude the security forces much longer had your men not come along when they did."

Carpenter nodded, but said nothing.

Ezekiel cleared his throat, drawing Carpenter's intense gaze. "Matthew and I were discussing a plan."

"A plan?" Carpenter shifted from one foot to the other.

"Yes, to prove Matthew's innocence."

"And you are certain of his innocence?"

Before Ezekiel could comment, Matt asked, "If you are not, why would you offer me safe passage and a place to hide."

"Whoever assassinated the president could only be considered a friend of the Alliance, Mr. Kelly. Whether you pulled the trigger or not, these men look at you as a hero." Gesturing with an open hand, he waved his arm in a wide arc, indicating the fifteen or so men who filled the small apartment.

"Well, as much as any man wants to be a *hero,* I didn't do it. And, until I can prove it, I don't hold much hope of being able to go back to my own time."

"Quite the contrary, Mr. Kelly, we have the means to send you home tonight. Once you're back in your time, you will be as free as a bird, I believe the expression goes."

"I won't go back without Kate."

163

Nancy Fraser

"Why not?" Carpenter asked. "In all likelihood, Arianna or Daniel will jettison her off on the first time shuttle available."

"Why would they do that?" Matt asked.

"Your wife is a very intelligent woman who, I suspect, will not let things be until she finds you, or someone on whom to blame the president's demise. Mrs. Westmoreland, through Daniel of course, now rules the world. Kate Kelly will only complicate Arianna's reign."

"But—" Matt began, only to be interrupted.

"If you will excuse me, Mr. Kelly, I have a previous engagement." As quickly as he'd arrived, Rohn Carpenter departed.

Matt watched as the man made his way through the throng of men, speaking to one, shaking hands with another: a consummate politician with just enough rough edges to make him the opposition to whoever held power. Yet, something in the way he held himself gave Matt the impression there was more to the leader of the Alliance than met the eye.

Once Carpenter had exited the apartment, Matt let out a long sigh. "I don't know about you, Ezekiel, but I'm in bad need of some sleep."

"It is a good idea that you get some rest. Tomorrow we will make contact with Kate and you two can work out the details of your investigation into Westmoreland's murder."

"Then you don't believe I did it."

"Of course not," Ezekiel stated firmly.

Most of the men had left shortly after Carpenter, leaving behind a small contingent of personnel to guard the Alliance's safe house. Intent on finding himself a place to rest, Matt almost missed Ezekiel's soft spoken entreaty.

"Matthew."

"Yes, what is it?" Matt drew a hand over his face, rearranging his fatigue.

"There is something I need to tell you."

Something in Ezekiel's expression spoke to Matt in ways which went far beyond uttered words. In Ezekiel's eyes he saw a mixture of fear and shame, the combination piquing his curiosity and igniting his uneasiness. Somehow, Matt knew he wasn't going to like what he was about to hear.

Ezekiel sighed and began speaking, "It was not an accident of fate that brought you and Kate to us. Well, actually *you* were an act of fate. Kate's transportation was intentional, just as she suspected."

"Why? What has Kate done to deserve being brought here?"

"It is not what she has done, but what she was not allowed to do."

"I don't understand."

"It was the Alliance's intention to right a grave injustice. We were going to bring Kate forward in time and then return her through another window three years earlier."

"Three years," Matt repeated. A sudden knot tightened his gut and he closed his eyes to fight back the memories. "I thought you said we had to go back to some square on a grid."

Ezekiel stared at the ground rather than face him. "It is what I was told to say. The truth is, we can send you wherever we need to."

"And, what about the injustice you mentioned?"

"Kate never should have lost her baby."

An invisible hand twisted the knot a little tighter. "Go on." Although his words came out calm, he felt anything but.

"Travellers from our time went backward to murder Kate's baby, your baby. They drugged her mineral water with something untreatable by your doctors, thereby changing history to their advantage. It was our intention to correct their alteration by reinstating Kate's pregnancy and then guarding the time portal so the assassins could not accomplish their task a second time. I am sure our plan would have worked had you not shown up at Madame Olga's unexpectedly and then, during the transportation sequence, refused to release Kate's hand."

"Why was it so important to the Alliance to save our baby? And how would it have changed history?"

"Sean Patrick Kelly, your son, was going to be president. That is why Westmoreland had him killed."

FOURTEEN

Kate sat at the desk in the sitting room of her suite and reviewed the list she'd made early that morning. A chronological listing of every event, no matter how trivial, from the time she arrived at Madame Olga's up until Matt had left to speak to the president, lay spread out on the desk before her. As she reviewed each event, she placed a checkmark next to it. She'd completed the exercise so many times it had become nearly impossible to read the list because of the checkmarks. As an exercise in futility, this one seemed to rank right up there with trying to forget her ex-husband.

About to return to the list for yet another review, she was saved from the task by Esther's arrival. "Good morning, Kate Kelly."

"Good morning, Esther." Pausing barely a heartbeat, she asked, "Is there any news of Matthew's whereabouts?"

"None, I am afraid. The security forces have been claiming his capture all night long but, so far, they have produced nothing. I am certain your husband is still out there somewhere."

Kate expelled a sigh of relief. "I am certain, if I am allowed to examine the crime scene, I can help the security people in their investigation."

"The *crime scene*, as you call it, has been searched thoroughly. As we speak, the maintenance staff are in the process of cleaning the room and preparing it for Daniel's use."

"They're cleaning it! Are they crazy? They can't do that. At least not until I've had the chance to prove Matt's innocence. I must be allowed to examine the room before it's cleaned."

"I am afraid it is too late. It is not likely you would have been granted permission since the evidence is so strong against your husband. He has already been tried and convicted."

"He's not even here. How can they convict him if he's not here to defend himself?"

"Our justice system works far differently than yours, Kate. We review the data, feed it into the computer, analyse it and come to conclusions."

"But that's ridiculous, not to mention unfair."

"I am sorry, Kate, there is nothing either you or I can do."

"If they are so sure of Matt's guilt, what harm could there be in my looking at the crime scene?"

"I will ask permission, if that is what you want."

"It is definitely *what I want.*"

Esther stepped forward until the two women stood toe-to-toe. In a hushed whisper, she told Kate, "In the meantime, you must do something for me."

"Which is?"

"You must wear this crystal pendant around your neck. Never take it off."

"Why?" Holding the pendant at arms-length, she studied the crude setting and leather strap. "What is its purpose?"

This time Esther sighed deeply and closed her eyes in apparent contemplation. "It is a divinity stone."

"Is that something religious?"

"No, not divinity as in a deity but, rather, as in divination. It is used to help people communicate telepathically."

"Sorry, I don't believe in all that hokus pokus stuff."

Esther smiled serenely and, taking the necklace from Kate's hand, she set it in place around her neck. "I would almost guarantee that, up until a few days ago, you did not believe in the ability to travel through time either."

The stone, so cold in her hand, felt warm where it lay against her chest. Without thinking about what she was doing, Kate closed her hand around the stone. The gemstone grew warmer and, when she released it, it seemed to glow with an internal light.

"See, Kate, you already know how to use the stone."

"No, I don't." Yet, deep inside, she somehow understood exactly what would be expected of her.

"Matt will be given a crystal just like yours. When the time is right, he will contact you. Telepathically of course. Remember, it is not necessary to speak the words out loud. As a matter of fact, it could be dangerous if someone were to overhear."

"How do you know all of this?"

"It is an inherited trait. One that dates back many centuries in my family. Madame Olga was my great-grandmother."

"Really?"

"Yes, really."

"Is that how Ezekiel and Madame Olga became, ah, travel associates?"

"No, that is not how it happened." Pointing toward the sofa on the opposite side of the room, Esther confessed, "Perhaps we should sit down. It is time I told you the truth about why you were brought here."

****

Kate stood beside the desk where the president had been assassinated. There wasn't much left to examine. Yet, she inspected the area inch-by-inch in hope of finding a clue. Somewhere, deep within, she wasn't sure why she bothered. No matter what she found, she stood very little chance of being believed. Especially considering the overwhelming evidence the security people had amassed implicating Matthew.

Then, she thought of their son, and of how he'd been murdered by Westmoreland's henchmen. She felt no remorse for the president's death. If anything, he probably deserved to die. However, even if Matt had known about what Westmoreland had done, he wouldn't have murdered the man. Not Matt. He would have sought justice in another way. If for no other reason than to prove Matthew's innocence, she had to find something.

"I want to see the body," she announced suddenly, startling both Esther and the security guard who had escorted them into the room.

"That is not possible," the man told her. "The president's body is being prepared for burial."

"It is imperative I see the body," Kate repeated. "Surely, if your mathematical system of justice is so accurate, there could be no harm in my viewing the president's remains."

The man only glared at her, his cold and calculated stare sending a shiver down her back. "Come with me. I will ask permission of my superiors."

"Kate," Esther whispered as they negotiated the narrow hallways leading to the lower floors of the government building. "Are you sure you want to do this?"

"If it will bother you, Esther, please do not come with us. I have seen more than my share of dead bodies. I can handle it."

They arrived outside an unmarked room. The guard placed his hand against the security panel and the door slid upward. "Come on, Mrs. Kelly, let's get this over with."

Kate stepped into the room, followed by the

guard and then Esther. On the far side of the room a
man, most likely a modern day mortician, worked on
the burial preparations.

"May I?" Kate asked, reaching for the sheet that
covered Westmoreland's head.

The man, rather than respond, stepped back and
allowed her the requested access. She wondered if
he'd answer the questions she was certain to ask.

With her hand shaking far more than she'd
expected, Kate drew back the sheet. The president's
face had obviously been washed clean of blood, yet
the bullet holes shone prominently against his pale
skin. "Is there an exit wound for each of these
entrance wounds?"

The mortician looked to the guard for
assistance. The guard nodded, indicating that he
should answer. Kate breathed a sigh of relief.

"All but one seems to have exited the president's
body. I suspect there is one bullet buried in his lung.
There doesn't seem to be any reason to remove it,
considering how any of the other five wounds could
have killed him."

"Were the spent bullets recovered?" she asked.

This time the guard answered. "Two bullets
were removed from the chair behind the president.
Two more were found on the floor. The fifth bullet
was never found."

"And the bullets all matched?"

"Yes."

"Could I see one of them?"

The guard nodded and the mortician crossed the
room to his desk, opened a drawer and brought out a
clear glass container. Inside were four bullets. She
didn't need to examine them to know they came from
a 9mm Beretta. She'd seen this type of bullet
hundreds of times before. She'd watched Matt
remove them from their clip and hold them in his
bare hand, examining each for defects before

replacing them and then returning the clip to the gun. If nothing else, Matt had always been thorough.

"How about the gun? Did you retrieve the gun?"

"No," the guard told her, "yet your husband was the only one who owned such a weapon. And, when we checked the president's desk, where your husband's gun was supposed to be, it wasn't there."

"Still," Kate pointed out however futile, "without a murder weapon, all you have is circumstantial evidence."

"I do not know what you mean by *circumstantial* evidence. We have our data, and it has been analysed. Your husband has been tried and convicted. And, as soon as he's found, he will be executed."

Rather than allow this horrid man to see he'd upset her, she turned back to the president's body and pulled the sheet down to reveal all of his chest. The wounds were larger than the ones in the president's head but Kate knew that was attributable to the larger expanse of the body, rather than hope there could have been another weapon. These wounds had as yet to be cleaned and she picked up the magnifying glass beside the table and leaned closer. The outside of the wounds were ringed in black, indicating the shots were taken at close range, leaving behind—

"Could we go now?" she asked suddenly.

The guard, clearly confused by her sudden change of heart, shrugged his shoulders and motioned her forward. "Thank you for your time," she told the mortician.

He nodded and then returned to the job of preparing the president's body to lie in state.

"Powder burns," Kate explained when she and Esther were alone.

"Powder burns? I do not understand."

"The killer will have residue from the gun on his

hands. Possibly even beneath his fingernails and embedded into his clothes."

"But surely, by now, he will have washed his hands."

"Yes, but unless he's familiar with this type of gun, he might not have taken the time to clean beneath his fingernails. And, you said yourself, the clothing of today was made for extended wear and is not laundered as frequently as we do in our time."

"So, if the killer has not cleaned his clothing, we can find him. But how? Surely if he notices these, powder stains, he will wash his clothes."

"The residue is minute. Often not visible to the naked eye unless it is as concentrated as it appears around the wound. Many a criminal has been brought to justice based solely on an inspection of his clothing."

"But how do we inspect everyone's hands, fingernails and clothing?" Esther asked.

"That's where I'm stumped."

"Stumped?" Esther repeated, obviously confused by Kate's chosen jargon.

"Confused. Dismayed. It's the part I haven't worked out just yet. But I will."

"If it is at all possible, I believe you will find a way to clear Matthew's name."

"Then you believe he is innocent."

"Yes," Esther told her reassuringly, "I believe."

****

Kate worked until well past midnight, compiling notes, reviewing them and then making checklists of things she would need to do the next day. By the time she slipped into her sleeping clothes, she felt drained. Thoroughly spent.

She climbed beneath the lightweight sheet of the narrow bunk and rolled onto her side. Within moments she was fast asleep.

Something woke her from her sound sleep. Yet,

when she sat up in the bed and concentrated on listening, she could hear nothing and saw even less.

Then she felt it.

Against her chest, the divinity stone felt warmer than usual. When she looked down, it seemed to pulse with light. Closing her eyes, she grasped the gemstone in her hand and waited.

"Kate. Kate are you there?"

"Matthew. Is it really you?"

"Yes. Oh, God, Kate, I can't believe this is really happening? That this damned thing really works."

"Me either. Yet, I'm not about to let go of this rock and take the chance of losing you. Where are you?"

"I'm in a safe house that the Alliance has on the outskirts of what used to be Greenwich Village. I can't identify all of the landmarks, but I can't be too far from what used to be Madame Olga's home."

"Maybe the close proximity isn't just a coincidence. Maybe it has something to do with my transportation."

"Listen, Kate, there's something you should know about—"

"Esther told me."

"I'm sorry, Kate. It's my fault things didn't go as planned. If I hadn't been so damned stubborn about not letting go of your hand, we would both be back home now."

"We'd still be married. I'd still be pregnant."

When Matt didn't respond immediately, she feared they might have lost their telepathic connection. Grasping the stone tightly in her hand, she whispered, "Matthew. Are you there?"

"Yeah, Cricket, I'm here."

"What happened?"

"Nothing. I guess I just lost my train of thought for a moment."

"Try not to get derailed again, Matt. We need to

sort this all out."

"What do we have so far? I'm sure you've got checklists coming out of every pocket of your simtaki."

"Very funny."

"I'm not laughing, Cricket."

"Me either. I examined the scene of the crime."

"Me too."

"You did? When? How'd you get in?"

"I was there, Kate. The night he was killed. I discovered his body just minutes before Ezekiel and Daniel arrived. I knew as soon as I saw the first bullet hole, my gun had been used to assassinate the president. It didn't take a rocket scientist to figure out I was being framed. The only thing I can't figure out is by whom."

"Well, I got a chance to look at Westmoreland's body. They'd already cleaned up his face and throat, but his chest hadn't been worked on. There were two very prominent bullet holes. And, powder burns."

"Powder burns. That could be something. I could give myself up, they could check for residue. That would put me in the clear."

"No."

"No?"

"It stands to reason you'd know about the residue. You'd also know how to protect against it or dispose of it. Clearing you won't depend on your not having signs of gun powder residue but, rather, on who does."

"And just how do we go about finding the guilty party?"

"That's the part I'm still fuzzy about. I was hoping you'd have some suggestions."

"The residue will be detectable by ultraviolet scan. The only place they still use ultraviolet materials is in the data storage rooms for fingerprint identification."

"Some secured areas use it as well. That was

how the guard got me into the morgue, by palm scan.

If we could find a way to scan anyone who might possibly have had access, motive or opportunity, we might just hit the jackpot."

"First, we need to make a list of suspects."

"You mean you haven't already made one?"

"Well, yes, but I'm not sure how complete it is. After all, I don't know anyone outside this building other than Ezekiel and Esther. And, given the time of death, we can automatically eliminate Esther and Arianna Westmoreland. They were with me. Ezekiel was with Daniel. That leaves only you, and those people I've not been able to identify."

"Okay, Cricket, let's divide up the work. You work on a plausible security reason for the scanners. With Ezekiel's help, I'll compile a list of people we want scanned. And, assuming Ezekiel will be present for the scanning process, I'll instruct him as to what he should look for and what he should expect to find."

"And I'll see what I can find out about the staff on the inside. Maybe I can get a lead on who, besides the obvious, would benefit most from the president's death."

"Good idea, I'll do the same out here."

They fell silent for the briefest of moments. It seemed as if they'd used ten times the energy it should have taken for a normal conversation. Against her chest, the stone began to cool.

"Matthew."

"Yes, Kate?"

"You're a good cop. A great detective. You'll figure this one out soon and then we'll be able to go home."

"And you, Cricket, are an amazing woman."

"You're right, I am. Thanks for noticing."

"Goodnight Kate."

"Goodnight, Matthew."

Kate released the stone and laid her fingertips against her lips.

"I love you." The whispered declaration meant on for herself, reverberated against her skin.

FIFTEEN

Kate showered and dressed quickly the next morning. She needed to meet with Arianna and Daniel in order to put her plan into motion. A plan that had kept her awake for hours after she and Matt had stopped talking. Thinking. Whatever they were doing. Her brain still could not assimilate the strange phenomenon of telepathic communication.

Her breakfast had been delivered while she showered and she made a quick inspection of the contents of the tray. Rehydrated eggs, two slices of bread made from heavy grain and millet, juice from a fruit whose name she couldn't remember and coffee. Strong coffee. Just the way Matt liked it. The thought brought a lump to her throat. When she thought of Matt, her hand went automatically to the pendant hanging around her neck.

What if she couldn't convince Arianna that she and Daniel were in danger? What if, after all hers and Matt's efforts, they were unable to clear his name?

"Good morning, Cricket."

It wasn't until Matthew's greeting intruded on her thoughts that she realized she still held the stone tightly in her fist.

"Good morning, Matthew."

She drew a deep breath and released it in an effort to calm her pounding heart and clear her thoughts. She couldn't let Matt know how much she feared failing him.

"Are you up and dressed?"

"Yes, how about you?" The thought of Matt being

undressed and *up* set her pulse to racing.

"Tsk, tsk, tsk. Such wicked thoughts, Cricket. How will we ever solve this case if all you think about is sex?"

"Very funny. What have you discovered so far"?

"Only that I kind of like communicating this way. It's much easier than talking, something we were never very good at."

"Yes, well…" She shut her eyes and waited. Surely Matthew would sense her unease and change the topic of conversation. Thankfully, he did not disappoint her.

"I'm expecting Ezekiel at any moment. I'll tell him about our thoughts on the powder burns and I'll ask him if there's any way we can inspect the suspects, without being obvious."

"I've asked for a meeting with Arianna and Daniel. I figure, if I can convince them there might be another threat of danger, they may see the need for increased security."

"Be careful, Kate. And watch them for some sign of conspiracy. While neither of them can be identified as the shooter, it doesn't mean they didn't have a hand in this. If they totally disregard concern for their safety, it might mean they likely know who the killer is and have no reason to be afraid."

"I'd come to the same conclusion myself. Yet, as you say, we have to be subtle."

"Which means, my fiery-haired wife, you can't go losing your temper."

"Ex-wife."

When Matt didn't immediately respond, she felt a rush of remorse for her insensitive thought.

"Yeah, right. Ezekiel's just arrived. I'd better go. I'll talk, uh, think to you later."

"Matthew?"

"Yes, Kate?"

"Be careful."

Kate released her death grip on the stone. It fell against her chest and cooled quickly. Suddenly, she felt as cold as the lifeless crystal and more empty than she'd felt since the night Matt had moved out of their apartment. More alone than she'd felt when the judge's gavel had decreed their marriage over and done with.

There were a number of things she regretted in her life, but none of them more than losing Matt. More precisely, of chasing Matt away because of her inadequacies. She needed to clear his name and, in doing so, possibly make amends for some of her mistakes.

The unappetizing breakfast quickly forgotten, Kate crossed the room and ordered the door to the suite open. The moment the metal sentry slid upward, she came face-to-face with a somber-faced guard. Obviously, the man didn't want to be there any more than she wanted his close scrutiny.

"I would like to speak to Mrs. Westmoreland and Daniel."

"How convenient," the man said, his tone overtly sarcastic, "that's exactly where I have been ordered to take you."

****

Matt waited until the door had closed behind Ezekiel before he asked, "Were you able to find the necessary equipment?"

"Infra-red scanners are not often used, except in areas where we have not bothered to update the facilities. I have brought a model from storage. I do not know if it will work."

"Let's hook it up and take a look."

"What is it you intend to do with this scanner, assuming it is operational?"

"I intend to teach you some early twenty-first-century detective skills."

"Me?" Wariness tempered Ezekiel's obvious

curiosity.

"Yes, you."

"But—"

"While we're hooking up the scanner," Matt suggested, interrupting Ezekiel's confusion, "I'll explain."

Ezekiel removed a square-shaped box about the size of a shoebox from its padded carrying case and set it on the table in front of them. Then, he took what appeared to be a battery pack from his pocket and attached it to the scanner.

"Power programmer," Ezekiel explained.

"You read my mind," Matt admitted, although the thought made him uneasy.

"You are intensely curious, Matthew, although you are not as inquisitive as Kate."

He felt a moment of melancholy wash over him. He wondered how Kate was doing. Did she miss him half as much as he missed her? Along with his feelings of longing, came the double-edged sword that had always been part-and-parcel of their life together. What possible trouble might Kate have gotten herself into while trying to help him out?

****

"What do you mean you're sending me back home today?" Kate rose from the chair she had just taken and stormed across the room, planting herself firmly in front of the president's—Daniel's—desk. "You can't. I won't go."

"We can, and you will, Kate Kelly."

"But what about Matthew?"

"Mr. Kelly's fate is sealed. Once he is found, he will be executed."

"Couldn't you just send him back? I mean, can't something be done to change what has happened?" This tactic, this bargaining, was about as far from her plan as she could get. Yet, if she were sent home it would be impossible to help Matthew. If they could both be sent home, or history altered, as her life and the life of her baby had once been manipulated, then she would be willing to do whatever was necessary to save Matthew.

"We had thought of that," Arianna admitted from her seat at Daniel's side. "However, our advisors have suggested that, perhaps, history has been tampered with far too much already. That is why we are sending you home."

"Couldn't I at least stay to pay my respects to your husband?"

"Although it is very thoughtful of you, Kate, there are many political reasons why your presence would be unwise."

"Political?" Kate queried.

"It is common knowledge my husband had lost favor with a great majority of the people. We are hoping this tragedy can reunite the country into one, strong group. To allow the wife of my husband's assassin—"

"Alleged assassin," she felt compelled to point out.

"Your husband has been tried and found guilty, Mrs. Kelly," Daniel reminded her for what seemed like the umpteenth time.

"By your analytical system perhaps, Daniel, but not—"

"Mrs. Kelly," Daniel said sternly, drawing himself up to his full five-foot-five for emphasis, "by unfortunate circumstance, I am now the interim president. I would appreciate being addressed appropriately."

Kate could feel her composure slipping. She wanted nothing better than to tell Daniel Westmoreland that he would get her respect when, and if, he earned it...or, when he was old enough to shave, whichever came first. Instead, she swallowed her pride and said, "I am sorry, Mr. President.

Please accept my apologies."

"As I was saying," Arianna began again, "to have you present at my husband's funeral would only give the government's opposition something to rally around. It is better if they see we have dispatched you back to your own time. Then they will understand how serious we are about finding your husband and bringing him to justice."

"My husband will not take kindly to my being sent back," Kate told them. Behind her back she crossed her fingers for luck and hoped her spur-of-the-moment idea wouldn't backfire. "As a matter of fact, he might seek some sort of retribution."

"Retribution?" Arianna questioned.

"How?" Daniel asked, concern clearly clouding his young features.

"Working under the assumption that your data is correct, and my husband did assassinate the president, the gun was never found, which could mean Matt still has it." Kate sighed deeply, loudly, then set her gaze on Daniel's face. "A Beretta fires twelve bullets. Six for your father, and six—" Shrugging, Kate turned away and prayed that Daniel would take the bait.

"He would never get past our security."

Kate swallowed back the lump of apprehension she could feel forming in her throat. "He already has. He managed to get out of the government building undetected, didn't he?"

"Surely he wouldn't try to get back inside." Arianna's concern was suddenly as apparent as her son's.

"My husband is an expert in undercover surveillance. Disguises. I have no doubt he could get to me if he wanted."

"That is impossible," Daniel shouted. "Our security is—"

"Inept," Kate stated firmly. "They rely on photo

identification badges and travel in groups. As long as you are walking in a group, and the first person in the group accesses the locked door, any number of people can walk in." Pressing her point, she added, "I'd almost bet anyone will be able to access the funeral, especially if you are using the proceedings as a political gathering."

"It is not a *gathering*," Arianna insisted. "And we will have intense security."

"Well, then, if that is the case, there will be only a limited number of people admitted and my presence shouldn't be a problem. Surely, you can allow me to stay long enough to pay my respects to the man my own husband is accused of murdering."

"Very well, Mrs. Kelly," Daniel conceded all too easily, "you may stay until after my father's funeral. In the meantime, though, you will be placed on constant, personal surveillance. If your husband comes to within one hundred feet of you, we will catch him."

Kate felt her heart skip a precarious beat. "Exactly what is *personal* surveillance?"

"Something I am certain you will not enjoy."

That, she decided three and a half hours later, had been an understatement. Like something from her worst sci-fi movie nightmare, the electronic tether fastened to her wrist blinked with a series of red, green and blue lights in a random order so complex she couldn't begin to decipher their sequence. Not only did the tether keep her confined to her suite but it also monitored her heart rate and breathing pattern. Would the monitor also be able to read her emotions? Her thoughts? Would her *conversations* with Matthew be detectable?

If being tethered weren't bad enough, every hour on the hour, an extremely unpleasant man came to reset the damned thing. Did they really believe her capable of unlocking their mathematical jail cell?

Somehow, she didn't think so. If anything, the man's presence was obviously meant to be the *personal* part of the surveillance and intended to unnerve her. Despite her usually strong resolve, their ploy was working.

She checked her watch and confirmed she had less than fifteen minutes before the odious man returned. Would that give her enough time to contact Matthew? Or, should she wait until after the man's next visit? Kate grasped the stone in her hand and closed her eyes. Within seconds, the cool surface warmed. Her fingers tingled.

"Matthew."

As patiently as she could, Kate waited.

"Matthew."

Still no answer came and she could feel the first rush of nausea overtaking her. What had happened? Why wasn't Matt answering? Macabre images filled her head, visions of Matthew in the grasp of the government's security forces. Of Matthew's execution.

The door to the suite slid upward, startling her. Immediately, she released the stone and slipped the necklace beneath the collar of her blouse. When she turned to see who had entered, she was surprised to find Ezekiel and Esther in the company of the doctor who had treated her after her gunshot wound.

"Esther?"

"Kate," Esther began, "you remember Doctor Emerson don't you?"

"Yes, of course." A sense of foreboding came over her like a shroud. Why had they brought the doctor? Where was Matt?

"Hello again, Kate Kelly," the doctor greeted. "How have you been?"

Although she knew it was rude, she couldn't bring herself to engage in polite formalities when every one of her senses literally screamed *trouble.*

"Why are you here?" she asked.

"The sensors attached to your surveillance equipment have been indicating abnormal readings. After consulting with the technician that installed and adjusted your monitor, it was decided perhaps persons from your time are not capable of withstanding the electrical impulses given off by the equipment. Rather than risk anything else happening to you, I have been asked to remove the tether and provide you with a simpler form of surveillance."

"Which is?" Kate asked.

"We are going to implant a small transmitter beneath the skin of your forearm."

Kate shook her head. "No. I'll take my chances with the *impulses*. There's no way you're implanting some foreign object beneath my skin."

"But Kate," Esther reasoned, "it's for your own good."

"No."

"The sensors," Ezekiel explained, "are very sensitive. They pick up everything. Emotions often affect the readings. Thoughts. And, by ridding yourself of the tether, you will no longer require the technician's fine tuning."

The thought of being done with the man's hourly visits appealed to her, yet she hesitated. "I still don't understand why I have to be confined to this room by an electronic umbilical cord. It's not me the security forces are after, it's Matthew. If he were to find out about how I'm being held prisoner, he would be very unhappy."

"Perhaps," Ezekiel suggested, "that is the government's intention."

Her sigh was one of resigned acceptance. Despite her misgivings about the procedure, she knew she would do nothing that might endanger Matt any more than necessary. If Ezekiel was right, she'd become an unwilling pawn in the government's search. She just wished she could convince them they were looking for the wrong person.

"I have found out most unpleasantly what happens when I test the limits of the tether," Kate admitted. "What happens if I overstep the boundaries set by the implant?"

"Rather than the burn you have suffered to your wrist, you will receive a shock that will cause a sharp pain in your chest and produce dizziness which would make it nearly impossible for you to run."

Doctor Emerson's graphic description only increased her apprehension.

"And, when it is time to send me home, will the implant be removed?"

The doctor nodded. "Most definitely."

Kate reluctantly offered her shackled wrist for the doctor's inspection. "Fine, take this thing off and let's get it over with."

Ezekiel produced a computer card from his pocket and slipped it into the programming slot on the tether. The lights blinked their usual random pattern then stopped. The latch on the tether sprang open to reveal her wrist, along with the evidence of her stupidity. Esther's gasp, and the expression of horror on her face only made Kate more aware of her folly.

Doctor Emerson took her hand in his and turned it over, inspecting both sides of her wrist. "I will put something on this burn that should heal it within a few hours."

"What happened?" Esther asked.

"Isn't it obvious," Kate said, unable to keep the sarcasm out of her voice, "I tested the limits of the tether."

"But why?"

She couldn't answer. She couldn't explain what

had made her act so stupidly, so defiantly. At the time, defying the creepy little man and his computerized equipment seemed like the noble thing to do. Now, looking at the burn marks on her wrist, she felt stupid. Rather than respond, she only shrugged. When she met Esther's gaze, Kate realized her friend was on the verge of tears. It seemed almost as if Esther could feel the pain in Kate's wrist as distinctly as she did.

It is an inherited trait. One that dates back many centuries in my family. Kate thought of Esther's words, spoken so softly when she'd given her the necklace. Where Esther's strange powers physical as well as mental?

"We will need to wash this burn with an antiseptic lotion." As he spoke, Doctor Emerson opened the small, metal box at his side, withdrawing from it the lotion and a glass tube applicator. "We will place the implant in the opposite arm."

Kate sat quietly while the doctor tended to her burn. The lotion brought a welcome measure of relief.

"I cannot believe they left the bracelet on your wrist after the burn. They should have called me immediately."

Hearing the doctor's claim only reminded Kate of how her jailer had laughed when she'd stepped beyond the doorway in defiance of his orders. Despite the relief the antiseptic lotion offered, she could still feel the searing pain she'd experienced when the tether had beeped, flashed and flared.

"Well," she responded, again amazed at the sarcasm she couldn't hide, "some people just seem to enjoy their job too much."

"I am truly sorry," Ezekiel told her, his eyes glazed with tears just as Esther's had been. "This has all gotten so out of hand. It is all my fault."

Kate reached out with her free hand and laid

her palm against Ezekiel's cheek. Against her chest, she could feel the heralding warmth of the divinity stone.

Not now, Matthew. It isn't safe.

To Ezekiel, she said, "You were only doing what you thought needed to be done to right a terrible wrong." Offering him a compassionate smile, she suggested, "Perhaps, if you'd known how much trouble I can be, you might have thought twice about bringing me here."

Again the stone warmed and Kate's heart ached with the knowledge she would have to ignore Matt's beckon.

"Okay, Kate," Doctor Emerson said, releasing her arm. "You will soon be as good as new. For all our savageness in the way we monitor, at least our advanced medicine can quickly make amends." Taking her other hand in his, he continued, "let me get this implant in place and then we will leave you to rest."

"Yes, please. I believe I would like to take a short nap."

It took only a moment for the doctor to implant the monitoring device. As quick and as relatively painless as receiving a flu shot, the procedure went smoothly. When the doctor had finished, she looked down at her arm, unable to detect anything out of the ordinary.

"I will be leaving now. If there is anything you need, or if you have any abnormal side effects, please have security call me immediately. And Kate," the doctor added, his tone serious, "please do not test the limits of the implant. It is far more dangerous than a burn on the wrist."

She swallowed back the lump of emotion forming in her throat. "Don't worry, doc, I've learned my lesson."

When the door closed behind Emerson, Kate

turned to Ezekiel and in a hushed whisper, told him, "Matthew's been trying to contact me for the past few minutes. I need to respond."

"We will leave also. After you contact Matthew, it might be wise for you to replenish, as the doctor suggested."

"I will. I promise."

The moment the door closed behind Esther and Ezekiel, Kate gathered the stone in her hand and held it close to her heart. The stone warmed and she breathed a sigh of relief.

"Matthew."

While she waited for him to respond, she went into the sleeping room and turned back the covers on the bunk.

"Matthew."

Panic welled up within her chest when Matt failed to answer. Although she held the stone tightly within her grasp, the warmth was gone. She let the stone fall from her grasp.

Restlessness made her pace, from one side of the room to the other, back and forth, back and forth until shear exhaustion forced her to stop. She sat on the edge of the silk-covered mating bed and removed her shoes and socks. Her slacks pooled on the floor at her feet, followed by her blouse, bra and panties. Too exhausted to stand, let alone move to the bunk she'd prepared, she slid beneath the silk sheets. Within moments she was fast asleep.

****

"Hello there, sleepyhead. I thought you were going to wait up for me."

Kate rolled over in the big, king-sized bed and stretched out her arms. Matt slid into bed beside her, the feel of his warm, undeniably male body most welcome after a long, hard day. "How'd the stakeout go?" she asked.

"Zilch, nada, less than zero. They never left the

house the entire time." Matt drew her into his arms and pressed her head to his shoulder. "All I could think about was getting home to you." To prove his point, he captured her lips in a warm and tender kiss.

"Mmm."

"Mmm? All my kisses rate is an Mmm?" Obviously hoping for a different response, he deepened the kiss. As the kiss escalated, he slipped his fingers beneath the strap of her gown and closed his hand over her breast.

A loud thump drew Kate from her dream. Startled by the foreign sound, she sat up in the bed. The silk sheet fell to her waist and she gathered it up in one fist and held it in front of her. "Who's there?"

Not surprisingly, she received no answer.

She sat there quietly, listening for any indication she was not alone. No other sounds intruded on the tomb-like silence of the bedroom. After a few moments, she lay back down and smoothed the sheet over her body. The silk felt cool against her skin, a direct contrast to the heat her dream had created.

She took the stone in her hand and clutched it tightly.

"Matthew."

She waited.

"Matthew."

Tears rolled slowly down her cheeks and she made no effort to wipe them away. She tossed and turned long into the night, never once letting go of the divinity stone. Never once feeling its warmth against her palm.

"Where are you Matthew? Why don't you answer?"

SIXTEEN

Esther arrived early the next morning, waking Kate from her restless night's sleep.

"Good morning, Kate Kelly," Esther greeted.

Still ensconced in the big mating bed, she clutched the silk sheet in her fist and held it firmly to her throat. "Good morning, Esther." With her other hand, she pushed her hair from her face, and asked, "What time is it?"

"Six-thirty in the morning."

"Six-thirty? What in the world—" she began, only to be stopped short by the memory of not being able to reach Matthew. "Is something wrong? Is Matthew okay?"

"Nothing is wrong, Kate. We have a busy day ahead of us and I have come to prepare you."

"Prepare me?"

"Get out of bed, Kate. I will explain while you take your morning supplement." Esther turned and started toward the bedroom door, stopping only long enough to add, "After you have showered, dress only in your underclothing. I have brought suitable mourning clothing for you to wear to the funeral."

"The funeral is today? But, I thought—"

"There will be a day-long mourning period, followed by a state dinner and candlelight ceremony. Then, after the public has paid their last respects, the president's body will be removed for cremation. It will mean a long and tiring day. I hope you are up to it."

"I'll manage. I just hope everything runs smoothly."

"Yes," Esther agreed, "so do I."

Once Esther had left the sleeping room, she lay back against the bed, grasped the divinity stone in her hand, and closed her eyes.

"Matt?"

"Good morning, beautiful."

"Why the heck didn't you answer me last night when I called? I was worried sick."

"Good morning to you too, Matt."

"Dammit, Matt, don't get sarcastic with me. I barely slept."

"Sorry, Cricket, but I had my hands full last night."

"Full of what?"

"Now who's getting sarcastic? It just so happens, Ezekiel and I spent most of the night repairing the infra-scan machine. The two times you called me, I had company."

"What kind of company?"

Kate regretted the thought the moment she issued it. She could almost hear Matt's laughter.

"Nobody interesting, unfortunately. This place seems to be overrun with curious people. They all want a look at the man who shot Westmoreland. Nothing I can do or say will convince them they're looking at the wrong man."

"Today is funeral day. Arianna and Daniel insist they'll send me home as soon as the funeral is over. That doesn't give us much time to come with a miracle. I don't suppose you've come up with some sort of brilliant plan."

"Brilliant plans are usually your domain, Cricket. I do, however, have some good news."

Kate waited.

"Well? What is it?"

"Ezekiel received a call from Arianna late

193

yesterday afternoon. Whatever you said to her obviously spooked her, because she asked Ezekiel to arrange for computerized security at every entrance to the government building. What exactly did you say to her?"

"Basically, I lied. Or, possibly embellished a bit."

"Lied? You? Kate, your cheeks scream neon-red with even the smallest fib."

"And you're the only who knows about that particular trait. Anyway, I think both Arianna and Daniel were too worried to question my honesty."

"Worried about what?"

"Well, I sort of insinuated you'd be gunning for them if they tried to send me back in time without you."

"Oh, great, sweetheart. Just what I need, another APB out on my sorry butt."

"Don't worry, Matt, I'll be sure and recant my threat as soon as we've got this case solved."

When he didn't respond right away, she felt her stomach lurch. *Matthew?*

"I'm not sure it's solvable, Cricket."

"Of course it is. All we have to do is find the real killer."

She could hear Matthew's sigh as distinctly as if he were standing beside her.

"That's a mighty tall order, Kate. Mighty tall."

"Tall. Why didn't I think of that before?"

"Think of what, Kate?"

"I've got to go, Matthew."

"Kate?"

"I've got a hunch. I'll get back to you as soon as I can but, right now, there's something I need to do. I'm just not sure how I'll go about it."

"What's up? What have you got to do?"

"I need another look at the president's body."

Before Matt could respond, and possibly try to talk her out of her quickly-formed plan, she released the divinity stone and literally jumped out of bed. Within seconds, she'd gathered her clean underwear and headed toward the shower.

****

"So, Matthew, we are about to leave for the government building. You are sure you will be all right here on your own?"

Ezekiel's concern was evident, his anxious sincerity causing Matt to pause in his task of packing up the last of the infra-scan machines.

"I'll be fine, Ezekiel. After all, who do I have to worry about? Everyone will be at the funeral, won't they?"

"He is right, Ezekiel. You worry too much."

Matt turned to see Rohn Carpenter and his brother, Alan, coming toward them. Both men were dressed in dark clothing and wore the familiar leather wrist bands that bore the insignia of the Alliance.

"What is this?" Alan asked, pointing toward the infra-scan.

"It is an identification tool created long before you were born, little brother." Rohn pushed the younger man forward. "Here, stick your hand beneath the light and I will show you how it works."

Somewhat reluctantly it seemed, Alan did as he was told and Rohn nodded in Ezekiel's direction. "Engage the machine, Ezekiel. Show my brother how antiquated this equipment truly is."

Ezekiel flipped the switch. The light bar at the top of the machine flickered and crackled, drawing current from the power bar. When Alan jumped back in surprise, Matt chuckled and ushered the boy forward.

"Don't worry, Alan, it can't hurt you," Matt told him. "See, it, uh—" Matt stumbled over his explanation, his gaze drawn to Alan's hand where it rested beneath the scanner shield. Finally, he

195

finished speaking, "the scanner reads your fingerprint pattern and then processes your identification for clearance."

Rohn added, "The scanner is a grandfather to the single digit scanner and a great grandfather to the retinal scanner we use now. Isn't that right, Matthew?"

"Yes," Matt agreed absently, his attention focused on the unmistakable trail of gunpowder embedded in Alan Carpenter's leather wristband.

Kate selected one of the long, mourning dresses Esther had brought with her. The fabric, much smoother and softer than that of the simtaki, lay limp against Kate's skin. Shapeless, devoid of any decoration whatsoever, it reminded Kate of a black, floor-length pillowcase.

"This dress is downright ugly." Her bold pronouncement drew Esther's laughter.

"It looks no worse than my own."

She gave Esther's dress the once over. "That's true."

"The idea is to divert as much attention away from the mourners as possible. All eyes should be on the deceased, so that his image will remain in our heads forever."

"Speaking of the president's image, what do you think the chances are of my getting another look at the body? Before it is set out for viewing of course."

"In a term of your time, I believe the chances are slim to none."

"You learn jargon quickly."

"It is hard not to let some of your more colorful idiosyncrasies affect me. You are a remarkable woman, Kate Kelly. You dare to do things from which most women would run."

"Thank you. Still, if I could just pull off one more daring feat, I'd be a happy, remarkable woman."

"I do not know how we could make your request happen, Kate, but we will certainly try."

When Kate was dressed and ready to leave the suite, Esther ordered the door open and then asked the guard to come inside. "It is a necessary evil I am afraid," Esther explained, "that we must now tether you to the guard so your implanted surveillance device can be deactivated."

Kate nodded her understanding and then held out her wrist for the guard's electronic handcuff. Unlike the guards she'd become accustomed to, this man took his time with the tether installation, being extremely careful of her sore wrist.

"Is this okay?" he asked when he'd finished. "It is not too tight, is it?"

She met the man's gaze and shook her head, confirming by saying, "No. It's fine, thank you."

"Kate, this is Ulysses. He is Ezekiel's nephew. He will be your companion for most of the day."

"It's nice to meet you, Ulysses," Kate said sincerely.

Ulysses nodded, but did not answer.

Once Esther had called for deactivation of Kate's implant, the trio left the suite for the lower floors where the funeral would be centered. When Ulysses reached to activate the button for the second floor, Esther held out her hand and stopped him.

"We need to take Kate to the mortuary first."

"I do not have the type of clearance required for such a visit." Ulysses explained.

Kate couldn't help but notice that the young man seemed uncertain. Nervous. Nothing like the hard-edged guards to which she'd become accustomed.

"I don't want to cause anyone trouble, Ulysses," Kate said sincerely. "Yet, I can't leave any stone unturned when it comes to clearing Matt's name. Please take me to see whomever can grant me the clearance we will need."

"It is the least we can do," Esther added, "for the trouble our own selfish endeavors has caused both Kate and Matthew."

Ulysses reached once more for the elevator button. He hesitated, his hand hovering above the button for the second floor.

Kate held her breath in anticipation.

The young man sighed deeply and turned to Esther. "If it were anyone else asking, I would not put myself in such a predicament. However, I owe you and Ezekiel a debt I can never repay. I will do what I can to get us inside."

Ulysses pressed the button that would take them to the first sub-level. The moment they stepped out of the elevator they were met by two armed security guards. The weapons they carried looked extremely menacing. For a society which claimed no need for weapons of any sort, they certainly seemed to be familiar with their use. The sight of these obviously high-tech models caused Kate a moment of panic. Despite Matt's skill as an award-winning police sharpshooter, compared to these weapons, his Beretta, even if he had possession of it, would be no more protection than a child's water pistol.

"With any luck," Esther said suddenly, drawing Kate from her thoughts, "they will not have moved the president's body as yet."

"Somehow," Kate lamented beneath her breath, "luck hasn't been something I've counted on much lately."

Ulysses released her from the wrist bands binding them together and anchored the loose end of the electronic handcuffs to a nearby post. Confident she could not escape, he went to speak with the guards.

She found it difficult to stand still. Unlike the gentle Ulysses, the post refused to bend when she tugged. Her pulse raced at the thought of being shackled against her will. Stretching the tether as far as she could, she tried to close the distance between herself and the guards. She needed to hear what they were saying. Both men shook their heads repeatedly, looked only occasionally in her direction and then back at Ulysses.

Kate was about to abandon any hope of gaining access to the mortuary when Esther reached out and patted her on the arm. Kate met the other woman's gaze. Tears glistened in Esther's eyes and Kate suddenly realized how guilty Esther felt for all that had happened since their arrival.

Esther left Kate's side and approached the guards. They spoke for barely a minute when Kate saw the first guard nod his head. The second guard then used his thumb print to gain access to the restricted area. Within moments, she, Ulysses, and Esther stepped inside the dimly lit room. A single light shone at the far end. Beneath the light stood a large, glass tube at least seven feet high by four feet wide. Beyond the strange looking tube was the examiner's table. Peter Westmoreland's body, covered in what appeared to be a velvet shroud, lay on the table. Beside the table stood a rack similar to a gentleman's valet. A dark suit hung from the rack.

"Come on," Kate coached, starting forward and then stopping short when her tether tightened. Neither Ulysses nor Esther moved an inch. "I just need a minute. Please."

Esther and Ulysses exchanged glances and Esther nodded. She started forward again and, with obvious reluctance, Ulysses followed. Esther, Kate noticed, stayed three feet behind.

Once they'd reached the far end of the room, she moved closer to the table and reached for the end of the shroud. "Here, help me get this thing open." Again Ulysses hesitated.

"Please. It'll only take a minute."

Kate took hold of one side of the shroud in her free hand and Ulysses did the same. Together, they pulled the heavy cloth back to reveal Westmoreland's recently embalmed body. When Kate turned to thank Ulysses for his help, she realized his eyes were tightly closed.

"Please hold the shroud up to let the light in," she explained, "I'll just take a quick peek."

Within minutes they'd left the small, dimly lit room and made their way up to the grand hall where Arianna and Daniel held court and welcomed those who had come to pay their respects to the fallen president. Banquet tables were set out at both ends of the hall and held a vast array of foodstuffs and liquid refreshments. To Kate it seemed more like a wedding reception than a wake.

She crossed the room quickly, virtually dragging her *guard* behind her.

"I need to speak to you two," she said without preamble.

"We intend to speak to all of our guests," Arianna pointed out quietly.

"No, I mean I need to talk business."

"Business?" Arianna asked.

"Yes, as in monkey-business, set-up, charging the wrong man with your husband's murder."

"Just how many times do we have to go over this, Mrs. Kelly?" Daniel asked impatiently. "Your husband has already been found guilty."

"By some computer maybe, but not by logical thinking men and women who actually take time to look at the variables."

"Variables?" Daniel shot her an impatient glare.

Before Kate could respond, Arianna took hold of Kate's wrist and literally dragged her to one side and away from the crowd. Ulysses, she quickly realized, would have rather been anywhere other than in the middle of a confrontation between herself and the First Lady.

"Mrs. Kelly," Arianna began, her tone harsh, her gaze as cold as a marble headstone, "I am extremely tired of your attempts to discredit our government's criminal findings. Our system has evolved through years and years of technology that your time has not even dreamed of as yet. Isn't it enough you have made us so unsure of our safety we must resort to screening our guests before they can pay their respects to my late husband?"

"We may not have the advantage of your technological advances," Kate conceded, "however we do have human feelings and a commodity often far more reliable than technology."

"Which is?" Arianna asked, her voice dripping with sarcasm.

"Intuition. Gut reaction."

"If you do not mind, Mrs. Kelly, I would much sooner put my faith in the findings of our research. The cold, calculated printouts of our advanced computers, the *guts* of which are far more advanced than you can ever hope to understand."

"Hard-wired is not always foolproof. The data that comes out, even in your advanced society, is only as reliable as the data that went in. And, of course, the integrity of the person inputting the data."

"I guarantee you," Arianna said sharply, "the integrity of our security chief is beyond reproach."

Rather than argue the point, Kate asked, "Who is the head of security in charge of the investigation?"

This time, it was Daniel who responded to Kate's question. "The investigation would have ordinarily been conducted by Ezekiel but, do to his unusual friendship with Mr. Kelly, we turned everything over to Rohn Carpenter. He is the head of the Alliance party. His computer findings were then turned over to the high court. Three judges on the high court reviewed the evidence and declared your husband guilty."

"I would like to speak with Mr. Carpenter, and the three judges."

"That is not possible," Daniel told her.

"Why not?"

"Today is the day of my father's funeral, Mrs. Kelly. I insist you show him the proper respect and let your arguments rest. Maybe tomorrow—"

"Tomorrow will be too late," Kate explained. "Your father's body will be cremated and the most compelling evidence lost."

Daniel's weary sigh reminded Kate of her own level of frustration.

"Daniel," she said slowly, purposefully, "I know your father's death has touched you deeply. Despite your attempts to keep a strong front, inside you are hurting. That's the way I hurt for Matthew. I *know* he did not kill your father, and I can prove it if you'll let me."

"Even if the judges were to listen to your arguments, without another suspect it is highly unlikely they would reverse their decision."

"They can't execute an innocent man just because they don't have another lead."

"I will see what I can do to arrange an audience as soon as Mr. Carpenter arrives. However, do not get your hopes up, Mrs. Kelly."

"Thank you. All I ask is a chance to be heard."

A little over an hour later, the doors were opened in order to admit the general public to the great hall. A long, red carpet paved the way from the outside door to where the president would be placed for viewing. At the entryway, Ezekiel and another man oversaw the large and cumbersome infrared scanning equipment Arianna and Daniel had agreed to use to monitor the admittance of those wishing to pay their last respects.

Kate watched from a distance, hoping to catch a glimpse of something familiar, something that would add credibility to her arguments, should she ever be allowed to make them. One-by-one, the citizens of Ankara and Planet Earth filtered in, dutifully placing their hands beneath the scanners for positive identification. One-by-one, each received clearance from either Ezekiel or his young assistant.

"Who's that with Ezekiel?" Kate asked, her question causing Esther to turn and look toward the door.

"That is Alan Carpenter. He is Rohn Carpenter's younger brother. If he is here, Rohn cannot be far behind."

"Good. Perhaps, once he's arrived, Daniel can arrange for me to present my case, as limited as it is."

"You will do fine, I am sure, Kate. However, do not expect these men to be easily swayed. They do not take well to being questioned and would surely not wish to be proved incorrect."

"I wish Matthew were here. He'd know exactly what to do and how to proceed."

Once the visitors had been admitted, the doors were closed and locked. Much to her relief, Ulysses released the tether and allowed Kate her freedom. "I will not be far away," he warned. "Please do not test my generosity."

"Don't worry, Ulysses, I'll be on my best behavior."

She wandered around the large room, from one side to the other, consciously avoiding the end where the president's body had been placed for viewing. *Well, at least this explains the tall, glass tube.* Despite her supposed bravado in examining Westmoreland's corpse, there was something uncomfortable about seeing him standing there in full formal dress, backlit by mini- strobe lights that reminded Kate of her Aunt Hilda's aluminum Christmas tree. It was no longer clinical. It had now become emotional and, in some ways, almost comical in its absurdity. Whatever had happened to dignity? If this was how an advanced culture honored their dead, she'd be more than happy to return home to die.

The thought of returning home reminded her of Matt and of how important it was to clear his name.

Beneath the black mourning dress, she could feel the heat and weight of the divinity stone. Laying her hand against the front of the dress, she pressed the stone tightly to her breast.

"Matthew Kelly, you pick the most inopportune times—"

"I've never liked you in baggy black before, but that dress clings to all the right places."

Kate drew a quick breath. Turning a slow circle, she scanned the crowd in search of the man she loved.

"Where are you?"

"Not far, yet far enough. What have you got to tell me?"

"I've requested a meeting with the three judges and the security investigator that found you guilty. I hope I can convince them they're looking for the wrong man."

"What kind of proof do you have?"

"Not much, I'm afraid, and all circumstantial. If we only had the weapon. Or, more precisely, the shooter."

"I know who shot the president."

"What? You do? Who?"

"Mrs. Kelly?"

Kate turned to see who had dared interrupt her conversation with Matthew. Against her skin, the stone cooled quickly.

"Yes, Daniel, what is it?"

"The judges and Mr. Carpenter will see you now."

Daniel led her to an anteroom just off of the great hall. Three men sat behind a large oval table facing the door. A fourth man stood in front of a window which overlooked the main street adjacent to the government building. She could feel the heat of his stare immediately, his intense scrutiny made her instantly wary.

"Good afternoon, Mrs. Kelly," the man greeted, "we finally meet."

"You have me at a disadvantage," she said as calmly as she could manage, "since I don't know who you are."

The man stepped forward and extended his hand. After only a moment's hesitation, Kate held out her own.

"Rohn Carpenter at your service."

Carpenter's gaze seemed to assess her, judge her, and dismiss her. Defiantly, she countered with, "My husband's wrongful accuser."

"Our evidence shows differently, Mrs. Kelly."

Rather than respond, she turned toward the other men. "You gentlemen must be the high court judges."

"I am Jacob," the first man told her.

"And I am Saul," the second added.

"And I am David. What is it you wish to speak with us about, Mrs. Kelly?"

"I am hoping to prove to you that you are searching for the wrong man. I understand how your system of judgment is different from mine, but that doesn't make it foolproof. If you would only listen to my conclusions, and take them into consideration."

"I have studied the law for a number of years, Mrs. Kelly," the man named David told her, "and I have an avid interest in the laws of previous decades, previous centuries. This court, however informal it may seem, will not be duped by any trickery."

"I have no desire to trick you, only to convince you of my husband's innocence."

"Very well then, present your case."

"Okay," Kate said, nervously rubbing her palms against the skirt of the mourning dress, "I'll do that."

Rohn Carpenter took a seat opposite where she stood, his gaze breaking contact with hers only when she turned away to pace. With her back turned to him, Kate still felt the heat of his stare. The feeling was so vivid, so unnerving, that she wondered if all human beings of this century were blessed, or possibly cursed, with some sort of telepathic power.

"First, there's the evidence, or more precisely, the lack of hard evidence. You have no weapon."

"Since our century does not possess guns, as you know them," Carpenter interjected, "the weapon that was used to kill the president could have only been the one belonging to your husband."

"Yes, but the president took Matt's gun away the first day we were here. He locked it in his desk. How would Matt have gotten access to the desk?"

"The desk had been broken into," Carpenter countered. "If I am not mistaken, you examined the splintered wood for yourself."

"Yes," Kate agreed, "but, if the president was already in his office as your report claims then Matt couldn't have gotten to the gun. The gun had to have been removed before the president went into his office and before Matt got there."

"The president was not sitting at his desk when he was shot," Saul reminded her. "Mr. Carpenter's investigation showed the president was standing behind his desk chair at the time of the shooting."

"I know, and that brings me to my second point.

Whoever shot the president was shorter than he was by at least four inches."

"How do you know that?" Jacob asked.

"The angle of the wounds. The entry height of the first wound was roughly here," she told them, pointing to her own chest for emphasis. "However, the exit wound on the president's back was nearly four inches higher which would indicate the assailant was aiming upward. The same is true for the second and third shot. However, given the force with which the bullets struck the president, I believe it would be safe to assume that those first shots would have knocked the president off of his feet and possibly onto the floor or into his chair. The remainder of the shots were then fired and the angle reversed. Since President Westmoreland was barely five-foot-ten, my husband, at six-foot-one and a half, could hardly have been the shooter."

The judges conferred for barely a minute before asking, "Is there anything else?"

"There's also motive. What possible motive could Matt have had for shooting the president? I mean, technically, we were only going to be here for another day or so."

"Perhaps," Carpenter began slowly, precisely, "your husband did not like the travel arrangements."

"But that's the point. The calculations Daniel had quoted were wrong. Ezekiel had the correct calculations. He knew Matt and I could return together. Yet, we had been wrongfully led to believe the president's decision was final, giving Matt no alternative but to seek an audience with the president to argue our objections. I believe Ezekiel was told to give us this wrong information on purpose, forcing our hand and prompting my husband to seek out the president. Gentlemen, my husband was set up."

"But why, Kate Kelly?" Carpenter asked. "What

possible reason could anyone have for framing your husband?"

Kate felt her frustration mounting. "I don't know *why*, I only know he's been blamed for something he didn't do."

The judge who had introduced himself as Saul stood and came toward Kate, taking her hand in his. "Mrs. Kelly, it is no secret why you were brought here. Ever since Peter Westmoreland took office, the Alliance has been working diligently to find a way to oust him from power. When information surfaced that someone in his group of advisors might have used our advanced knowledge of time travel to, shall we say, eliminate his most likely political rival, they developed a rather unusual plan to correct this horrible crime. Your transportation should have corrected that wrong. Unfortunately, things do not always work out as we would like them. Often, good deeds, however misguided, only cause more trouble than they cure. Perhaps, your husband was aware of the circumstances surrounding your transportation and, in a fit of rage over the death of your infant, attacked the president."

"No," Kate denied firmly. "Matt didn't know about the reasons for our being brought here until after the assassination. He found out just shortly before me."

"Who told him?" Saul asked. "Who knows where your husband is hiding out?"

She remained mute, choosing instead to only shake her head. Nothing these men could say or do would make her betray Ezekiel or Esther, and especially not Matt.

"Mrs. Kelly," Jacob began, "I am afraid you have shown us nothing to sway our decision. If there is nothing else—"

"Powder burns."

"Powder burns?" Jacob repeated.

"Yes. You see, when a gun is discharged, at least a gun from the early twenty-first century, it leaves behind an invisible trail of fumes and minute particles which attach themselves to clothing and skin."

"If it is invisible, how can we detect it?" Carpenter asked, his tone bordering on outright laughter. "And surely you don't expect us to believe your husband would not have disposed of any such evidence by now."

"Of course he would have, had he been the assailant. However, since he isn't, perhaps the real killer hasn't thought to dispose of evidence he didn't know existed."

"Really, Mrs. Kelly, I do not believe—" Carpenter began, only to be interrupted by Saul.

"Just a minute, Rohn. I, for one, would like to hear how Mrs. Kelly plans to identify the alleged assailant."

"Well, sir, that's the part I'm kind of fuzzy on."

"Fuzzy?"

"I haven't got it all worked out just yet. I was hoping—"

"Mrs. Kelly, if you have no hard evidence to the contrary, I am afraid our decision will have to stand as is," Jacob told her. "We must get back to the great hall. It is extremely disrespectful for judges of the high court to be absent from the proceedings."

"But, if you'll just give me a few more minutes of your time."

"I am sorry, Mrs. Kelly, but there is nothing further to discuss."

The three judges stood in unison and walked to the door, each sparing one last glance in her direction. Behind her, Rohn Carpenter stood barely inches away.

"I am sorry, Mrs. Kelly. I am afraid your usually celebrated tenacity has not paid off too well.

However, perhaps you and I could get together in private and go over your ideas a little more intimately."

"I would sooner take my husband's place with the executioner."

The wretched man took one step closer then stopped short when the three judges, rather than exit the room, began backing up slowly.

"That's it gentlemen. If you'll just give Kate and me a moment more of your time, I think we can clear this whole thing up." The sound of Matt's voice drew her anxious gaze.

As the judges backpedaled past where she stood, she caught her first glimpse of Matt. In his arms he held a modified infrared scanner, it's usually steady stream of light flashing with menace and pointed directly at the men who had condemned him to die.

SEVENTEEN

Kate fought back the urge to rush forward and throw her arms around Matt in relief. Even though she felt certain the scanning machine was more flash than danger, she didn't want to jeopardize Matt's safety by catching him off guard.

"What is the meaning of this?" Saul demanded.

Matt pressed a button on the side of the infrared machine and the lights flickered brightly and then ceased. When he'd set the machine aside, Matt answered. "I've come to clear my name and, with the court's indulgence, provide you with the facts of President Westmoreland's assassination."

"Guard!" Saul shouted.

"The guards have been detained," Matt stated simply.

"All of them?" Rohn Carpenter asked, taking a step toward where Matt stood.

Kate took a step closer to Matt's side, uncertain of what help she would be, yet knowing she'd willingly put her own life on the line to protect him.

"Most of them," Matt countered, his gaze moving first to Carpenter and then sweeping the room and its other occupants.

When Matt's gaze met hers, she smiled. Yet, conscious of the hand Matt kept tucked inside his jacket pocket, she felt her smile fade.

When Carpenter took a second and then a third step forward, Matt withdrew his hand and produced the Berretta.

"If I were you, Carpenter," Matt said firmly, "I wouldn't come any closer." Waving the gun side-to-side for emphasis, he added, "Kate, maybe you'd better come stand by me."

Saul reached out his hand and held Kate back. "You see, Mrs. Kelly," the judge stated, "your husband *is* in possession of the weapon. Does that not speak of his guilt?"

"The *weapon*," Matt countered, "was discarded by the real killer and found by a member of the Alliance." Nodding toward where the judge held her arm, Matt suggested, "Release Kate and let her come to me. Then, we can sit down and hash this whole thing out."

Saul did as Matt requested, letting go of her arm and allowing her go to Matt's side. She approached cautiously rather than take the chance of blocking Matt's view of Rohn Carpenter and the others. When she'd reached the opposite side of the room, she brushed her hand across Matt's arm in an abbreviated greeting. Beneath her breath, she whispered, "You'd better have a *real* good explanation for the gun."

Matt's lips quirked in fleeting smile. Then, he leaned forward and spoke only loud enough for her to hear. "Kate, I'd appreciate it if you'd peek outside and let Ezekiel know we're ready for him."

She did as Matt requested, opening the door slightly and signaling to Ezekiel. Within moments, Ezekiel, Esther, Arianna and Daniel had joined them in the ante room. Once they'd all assembled, Matt suggested, "If you will all take a seat, we can get through this fairly quickly."

"This is ludicrous," Arianna cried, "and disrespectful to my husband's memory. The very thought of my being called away from my husband's funeral is shameful."

"My mother is right," Daniel added, "what will people think? How can we hope to recover from this tragedy if we lose the respect of the people?"

"If you'll bear with me for a few minutes," Matt explained, "justice, and your father's memory, will both be served."

"Very well," Saul stated, his authoritative voice convening an impromptu court. "We will give you fifteen minutes to present your case, Mr. Kelly. If you do not convince us of your findings, crude as they most certainly will be, we shall have no other alternative but to call upon Ezekiel and Rohn to take you into custody."

"I do not believe," Jacob added, "that, despite his friendship toward you, Ezekiel would defy our direct order to arrest you, Mr. Kelly."

"And I wouldn't expect him to," Matt countered, his response drawing the appreciative nod of the judges. "If, after I've presented my case, you still believe me guilty, I will surrender willingly."

Matt's words startled Kate. What if, despite his obvious confidence in his case, they didn't believe him? What if—

Suddenly, the thought of possibly losing Matt to this futuristic kangaroo court became far more real than she would have liked.

"Matt," she whispered softly.

Matt leaned forward yet kept his gaze on the room's anxious occupants. "What is it, Cricket?"

Kate swallowed hard and closed her eyes to gather her inner strength. Cupping her hand beside Matt's ear to shelter her words and keep them private, she admitted, "I love you. I always have and, no matter what happens, I always will."

"I know."

"You do?"

Matt gathered her fingertips in his hand and squeezed. "We'll talk about it later. Okay?"

She nodded and then backed away, giving Matt room and making him the center of everyone's focus.

"First off," Matt began, "it should be noted that I had no idea, prior to the president's assassination, that the death of our baby was due to a time-traveling murderer on a direct order from Peter Westmoreland."

Kate leaned back against the wall and watched the reaction of the assembled group. Only Daniel showed surprise at Matt's opening statement. Although he didn't comment, the young boy's complexion grew suddenly pale.

Matt continued. "I admit, when Daniel told me Kate and I were scheduled to be sent home separately, I left the data storage area and went to request a meeting with the president. *And*, I admit I was angry. But, not angry enough to kill the man. When I arrived at the president's office, the first thing I noticed was the lack of any type of security. In the past, when we'd been brought to see the president, guards seemed to be everywhere. In hindsight, I suppose my instincts should have sent me in another direction. Instead, I knocked and when nobody answered, I tried the door. Again, I found it surprising that the door was unlocked."

"Once I'd gone inside the office it didn't take long to piece together what had happened. Westmoreland was slumped over his desk and lying in a pool of blood. I checked for a pulse even though I knew he was dead."

"And how did you know that for certain?" Rohn Carpenter asked.

"In my twelve years as a cop, I've seen far more dead bodies than I care to count. Whether the eyes are open or shut, a dead man's face is like a mask."

"A mask?" Saul questioned. The tone of his voice held open curiosity.

"A mirror-like reflection of the person's last thought. Based on my experience, I'd surmise two things. First, the president knew his assailant and didn't fear him. And second, something the murderer said or did just prior to firing the first shots angered Westmoreland."

Again, Saul spoke. "Angered? In what way?"

"Judging from the way Westmoreland's eyes were not just open, but wide open, I'd say the murderer had told the president something he found hard to believe, something possibly even personal."

"This is ridiculous," Arianna said suddenly. "There is no way you can tell something like that from the expression on a dead man's face."

"Quite the contrary, Mrs. Westmoreland," Saul contradicted. "In the numerous crime reports I have studied, the ability to reconstruct details to within minutes of a crime are well documented."

"I still do not understand what all this has to do with Mr. Kelly proving his supposed innocence," Arianna returned. "It is only his word of what he saw against our evidence."

"You're quite right," Matt agreed, "however, there's more."

"It is not your opinion we seek, Mr. Kelly," Jacob noted, "but facts."

"After I made a cursory examination of the body, I examined the surrounding area. The first thing I noticed was the jimmied desk drawer. The very same drawer where Westmoreland had placed my gun. At that point, it didn't take a genius to figure out what was happening."

"Which was?" Carpenter asked.

"I was being framed."

"Why would someone want to frame you?" Daniel asked.

"The most obvious reason, of course," Matt explained, "was to get away with the crime. Also, who better to blame than someone who doesn't really exist in this world as you know it. Someone who, once executed, would have no effect on the day-to-day status quo. Someone, who could take the fall and not cause ramifications throughout the governmental system."

"All this conjecture, Mr. Kelly, is well and good," Jacob pointed out. "However, we need substantial evidence of someone else's guilt."

Matt nodded toward Ezekiel who took the infrared machine from where Matt had laid it and placed it on the table where the judges sat. With a flick of a switch, the machine sprung to life. Caught off guard, the men sat up suddenly and pushed themselves away from the bright light.

"One of the disadvantages of trying to frame me with my own gun is the fact that the murderer knew nothing about handguns, other than how to pull the trigger."

Matt's words were controlled, their very strength giving Kate a renewed sense of confidence. When Matt approached the blinking machine, she followed.

"As you can see, when I place my hand beneath the light of the scanner, nothing out of the ordinary appears. However...."

The sound of the Beretta being fired once, twice and then a third time made Kate jump, destroying every last ounce of her newfound security.

"Sorry," Matt apologized.

The solid pressure of Matt's hand against her back kept her steady when, all around her, the others were cowering for cover.

"As you can now see," Matt stated, once again placing his hand beneath the light of the scanner and waiting while the judges and guests regained their seats, "there are significant traces of gunpowder across my fingers and imbedded in the hair on the back of my hand." Turning his hand over and over, he told them, "it's what's called incriminating evidence."

"We are all aware of incriminating evidence," Jacob countered, his patience clearly tested by Matt's show-and-tell tactics.

"Feeling fairly secure in the fact that the true murderer would not know about the gunpowder, I began my search. I knew that if we used the infrared machine properly, the gunpowder might be detectable, assuming, of course, the shooter was unaware of how to rid himself of the residue. Ezekiel procured the first machine and, thanks to Kate, we were able to convince Daniel and Arianna of the need to beef up security around today's ceremonies. Then, quite by accident, while we were in the process of testing and setting up the equipment, we literally stumbled across a probable suspect."

"For a man so deep in hiding that our best security could not find him, you managed, Mr. Kelly, to communicate with a number of people. Including your wife." Jacob's comments, while somewhat skeptical in sound, held a hint of grudging respect. "I would be intensely interested in hearing how that particular feat was accomplished, especially given the fact Mrs. Kelly was wired with enough monitoring equipment to track the most minute ion particle."

Kate raised her gaze to meet Esther's before turning to face the assembled audience. "Perhaps," she suggested firmly, "I can shed some light in that area."

"By all means," Rohn Carpenter suggested sarcastically, "enlighten us, please."

"In our own time, Matt and I have worked together a number of times to solve crimes. Matt, of course, wanted to bring the perpetrator to justice. I, on the other hand, wanted to write a Pulitzer Prize winning story. We *know* each other. We anticipate. While I admit, I didn't know of Matt's gunpowder theory, I did know he would not give up until he'd found the killer. I admit, as much confidence as I had, and still have, in Matt's innocence, I was not altogether certain he wouldn't try something heroic, like showing up at the funeral. My suggestion for security was as much for Matt's benefit as for anyone else's. I'd actually hoped to keep him out of harm's way. Obviously, even I underestimated Matt's tenacity."

Judging by the expression on Rohn Carpenter's face, he didn't believe a word of her story. Arianna's countenance, on the other hand, drew Kate's curiosity and spiked her intuition to a higher level. "And," Kate added for emphasis, "it's no secret there is another underground government out there that would be more than happy to assist someone who might have a mutual dislike for the current government. Any one of them, and believe me I *never* reveal my sources, could have delivered messages between myself and Matt."

Jacob chuckled, drawing Kate's gaze. "Mrs. Kelly, you more than live up to our historical accounts of your tenacity. However, it is no secret you have been befriended by both Ezekiel and Esther. And, it is also no secret that Esther is gifted with certain abilities. How you and your husband have communicated is not important. The only important fact we have yet to ascertain is *who* killed the president, if not your husband."

Kate turned back to Matt, praying the finale of his speech would be as convincing as the beginning.

"As I said," Matt continued, "we discovered traces of gunpowder. They were imbedded in the leather wristband that is part of the uniform of members of the Alliance Party."

Both Ezekiel and Rohn reached for the wristbands concealed beneath the sleeve of their shirts. Kate felt certain, Ezekiel's movement was an unconscious one, although she harbored no such feeling for Rohn Carpenter.

"Tell us, Mr. Kelly, who is the guilty party?" Again, Rohn's voice bordered on sarcasm.

"That's where it gets a bit complicated," Matt admitted.

Oh, God, Kate thought, *please don't let it get complicated.*

"Immediately, I brought my findings and theories to Ezekiel and a number of his most trusted allies who then approached the person in question."

"Who," Ezekiel added, "had an airtight alibi."

"This is taking far too long," Arianna inserted bitterly. "I do not believe Mr. Kelly has shown us anything in the line of proof and, if he can incriminate no other person—"

"Oh, but I can," Matt interrupted. "When we questioned our suspect, he provided us with a reasonable explanation and viable alibi, as well as a few interesting pieces of information. Pieces that not only provide opportunity, but motive, as well."

"Who is this person?" Jacob asked.

"Alan Carpenter. Rohn Carpenter's brother."

Matt nodded and Ezekiel opened the door and had the guard bring Alan inside. The boy looked, to Kate, to be on the verge of tears, his nervous gaze jumping from his brother to Arianna Westmoreland and then to the panel of judges seated at the nearby table.

"Do you know who assassinated President Westmoreland?" Saul asked simply.

The boy nodded but said nothing.

Speak. Kate bit back the urge to shout the command.

"It is okay," Ezekiel assured the boy, "we will protect you. Tell the judges how you happened to be in possession of the incriminating wristband."

Alan Carpenter drew a deep breath and then closed his eyes before he spoke. "I found it just outside the government building. After word of the assassination reached the Alliance's headquarters, a group of us were sent out into the street to look for

Mr. Kelly. We decided to start at the government building and work our way out toward the harbor. Just outside the guard's door is a narrow alleyway. That's where I found the gun. Then, on the ground next to the refuse containers I found the other things."

"Other things?" Rohn asked.

Something in the tone of Carpenter's voice belied his usual forceful presence.

"Yes," the boy continued, "a pair of protective gloves, an identification card and the wristband. The gun and the gloves seemed to be discarded purposefully, almost as if they were intended to be found. The identification card had slid beneath the refuse container. I thought perhaps it had been dropped by accident. I am not sure about the wristband. Both the gloves and the identification card had blood stains on them. When I got back to headquarters, I ran the blood sample through the central computer system. As I suspected, it belonged to President Westmoreland."

"And, did you have the identification card decoded?" Jacob asked.

"No," Alan admitted. "Not at first."

"Why not?"

"I did not think it was necessary because everyone was saying that Mr. Kelly murdered the president. When Ezekiel and the others came to take me into custody, I admitted finding the gun. I was going to save it for a souvenir. And, I told them about the other things."

"Why did you hide this from me?" Rohn asked, his voice literally reverberating with anger toward his younger brother.

"I was afraid. I thought you would be angry with me for keeping the gun. Then, when I started believing Mr. Kelly's claims of innocence, I was afraid *you* might have been the one who murdered

President Westmoreland."

Kate, who had been watching Rohn closely, noticed the covert glance he gave Arianna Westmoreland. In turn, she realized, Arianna seemed to be holding her breath in anticipation of the young man's next words. A sudden thought occurred to Kate, a suspicion of collusion between the First Lady and the man considered to be the unofficial leader of the Alliance Party.

Alan's next words drew her back to his explanation.

"When Ezekiel took the identification card from me, I knew he would soon have it decoded. I asked to go with them to Central Records. I wanted to know for certain the card either was, or was not, my brother's."

"And was it?" Saul asked.

"No."

"Then, whose card was it? Who murdered the President?"

Alan pivoted slowly, his gaze moving from Rohn, to Matt, to Arianna to Ezekiel, stopping finally at the table where the judges held court. He closed his eyes and sighed deeply.

Kate sensed his fear. It took courage to do what had to be done. A courage few men possessed, let alone a young man barely older than the slain president's son.

Obviously seeking that courage in the deep breath he took, Alan Carpenter opened his eyes, lifted his arm and pointed. "The identification card belonged to him. Daniel Westmoreland."

EIGHTEEN

"That is impossible!" Arianna shouted. Protectively, she put her arm around Daniel's shoulders and drew him to her side. "Daniel would never—"

"I am afraid it is so," Ezekiel said softly. "The proof is there. If we were to load our database with the information we now have, the computers would most definitely conclude that Daniel murdered his father."

"But the computers would be wrong!" Arianna insisted.

"You said the computers were fool-proof," Kate reminded her, "and that the database had found Matt guilty. Are you saying the computers aren't reliable when it's someone you love who is being charged?"

Someone you love. Kate's own word echoed around her, sinking in to her subconscious. There would be no way to take them back. Nor, Kate realized, did she want to. She loved Matt. She always had and always would. No matter what happened when they got back home.

Matt met her gaze, his eyes flaring with the briefest of recognitions before the moment between them shattered with the sound of Daniel's voice.

"They are right, mother."

"Daniel?" Arianna's voice cracked, her well-honed political armour dented by her son's admission.

"I shot my father."

"But why?" Kate asked before anyone else could.

"It is complicated."

Kate felt a moment of compassion for Arianna as the woman laid a trembling hand to her mouth to stifle a cry.

"Perhaps," Saul suggested, "we should all take a seat and hear Daniel's reasoning before he is sentenced."

"Sentenced?" Arianna whispered. "No, please. Not my baby."

"I am not a baby, mother. Until my guilt was established, I was considered to be the heir to the presidency." Sparing a glance in Rohn Carpenter's direction and then turning back to his mother, Daniel asked, "Is this not what you and Mr. Carpenter were planning during your late night liaisons? Did you not plan to run the country as my advisors until I reached legal age?"

"I—" Arianna began, only to be interrupted by Daniel.

"It does not matter. I did not murder my father for your benefit, but for my own. I found out only a few weeks ago about my father's part in the assassination of Mr. and Mrs. Kelly's baby. I also found out about Ezekiel's plan to bring Mrs. Kelly forward in time and then return her in order to correct the horrendous thing my father did. If the Alliance were able to reverse history, my father would not be president. I would not be heir. The only logical thing to do was to change the present and frame Mr. Kelly so further alterations could not take place."

"Logical?" Kate gasped. "You call murdering your own father logical?"

Matt took hold of Kate's hand and pulled her close. In the shelter of his arms, she trembled.

"You do not understand, Mrs. Kelly. My father was a pawn. He had no real power. He was controlled by these men, these judges. They are the ones who condemned us to a new order, a new way of life. A life most did not want."

What Daniel said next made Kate weak.

"I have seen the history the way it should have happened, Mrs. Kelly. The way it would have happened if your son had become President. We would have had one less war and been far better off as a society with Sean Kelly as our leader."

****

Kate sank into the hot tub of herbal water, letting the horrible realization of all that had happened float slowly through her mind. Poor Daniel. His punishment had been swift and certain. His execution immediate. She felt a moment of sympathy for the grieving Arianna. She, too, had now lost a son to this strange and unforgiving world.

"Kate?" The sound of Matt's voice felt as soothing to her as the herbal waters. When he came through the door, her pulse quickened.

"I'll be out in a few minutes."

"We need to talk, Kate. Now." Matt knelt on the floor beside the huge tub. With a gentle nudge of his hand, he motioned her forward. Then, he took soap and cloth in hand and began washing her back.

"Matt, I don't think—"

"Then don't. Just close your eyes and listen."

Against Kate's chest the divining stone warmed. Kate lifted her hand from beneath the water and grasped the stone tightly.

"*I love you, Kate.*"

"*I—*"

"*No, don't say it. Not yet. There's something I have to tell you first. It's about the night our baby died. I was so wrought with grief, I couldn't think straight. I loved you so much. Yet, it was my fault. If I'd only been there, if I'd only kept our lunch date, it wouldn't have happened.*"

"*No, Matt, it still would have happened.*"

"*I made a vow that night. I swore I wouldn't let*

up until I'd found the killer. My bullheadedness was what broke us apart."

"No." She knew she had to correct him if they were to ever have a chance at reconciliation. *"It was my fault our marriage ended. I couldn't let go of my grief. Yet, I couldn't talk about it, not with you, not with a priest, not with a counsellor. I couldn't show my weakness. I couldn't let you down."*

"We let each other down, Kate."

Kate released her hold on the divining stone and turned to face Matt, coming up onto her knees beneath the water. Her wet hand pressed firmly to Matt's cheek, she told him, "Then I'd say we have a lot of making up to do, wouldn't you?"

Matt nodded.

"I love you, Matt. And, if there's any way on this earth, on our own earth, to make it happen, we're going to work this out. I promise."

"What if we can't?" Matt asked. "What if, when we get back, we don't remember a thing? We'll go back to our separate lives, both of us too damned stubborn to admit how much we care, or that we have weaknesses only the other can forgive."

Kate stood, the warm water sluicing off her body like a cascade of scented rain. Matt's gaze followed, warming her where the retreating water left her chilled.

"I'm not sure how we'll know," she admitted. "But I figure, if we sleep on it, we'll come up with a solution."

"Sleep?" Matt repeated, drawing her from the tub and into his arms.

"Maybe. Maybe not."

****

Kate awoke the next morning wrapped in a blanket of warmth created by Matt's embrace. No matter what happened when they finally made it home, last night had been the most wonderful of her life. If only there were a way. If only—

The sound of the overhead speakers clicking on drew her from her thoughts and Matt from his sleep.

"Good morning, Mr. and Mrs. Kelly," came the anonymous voice. "Morning supplement will be served in thirty-five minutes."

Matt groaned and rolled over.

"Come on sleepyhead," Kate cajoled. "Esther and Ezekiel will be waiting."

"Not enough sleep," Matt grumbled.

"It's your own fault."

Matt nuzzled his morning beard against her throat and growled deeply. "No, it's not."

She squirmed in Matt's embrace, wanting nothing more than to continue the lovemaking for which they had gladly forfeited their sleep, yet knowing today would be the turning point in both their lives. Today they were going home.

****

Less than an hour later, they stood on the same transport pods that had been used on their previous botched return. Kate eyed the lighted surface with trepidation. What if they failed again? She had no desire whatsoever to return to the Wild West.

"Are you sure this will work?" she asked.

"Yeah," Matt echoed, "are you sure?"

"Yes, we are sure," Ezekiel told them confidently. "All of the coordinates are set. You will be returned to your separate homes on the morning of your trip to Madame Olga's. You will go about your day, as you had done. Only, I will not come for Kate. I will not risk bringing you back to our world and putting you through all of this for our own selfish reasons."

"We'd hoped to find a way to be together again," Kate admitted. "Is there no way we can keep at least some of our memories? Surely, for as long as we've been here, we must be able to retain something."

"It would not be wise. We have been ordered to give you an injection prior to transportation to aid in your memory loss."

Esther's surprising pronouncement dashed any last hope Kate had of saving her marriage.

"I understand," Kate said softly. "I don't want to, but I understand."

They took their places on the transport pods and Ezekiel and Esther came to stand in front of them. Esther reached out her hand to Kate and explained, "I will need to retrieve the divining stones."

Reluctantly, Kate removed the stone from around her neck and laid it in Esther's outstretched hand. Kate watched as Matt, too, removed the divining stone from beneath his shirt and gave it to Ezekiel. In turn, Ezekiel handed Matt the gold watch he'd taken from him when they'd first arrived.

"According to this," Matt told them, glancing at his watch and forcing a hint of laughter into his voice, "it's six-thirty in the morning on December 16th."

"Yes," Ezekiel explained, "I have set it for your return. It will begin running again as soon as you reach your destination."

"Part of me doesn't want to go," Matt admitted. "If we were to stay here, Kate and I could be together."

"As good as that may seem to you, Matthew, your permanent displacement would alter history and things as we know it here would change."

Kate shook her head in genuine dismay. "Despite all I've learned, it's all still so confusing. It's—"

Her concerns were interrupted by the opening of the transport room doors. As Ezekiel had told them to expect, Saul and Jacob had come to oversee the transportation.

"Have you removed the implant from Mrs.

227

Kelly's wrist?" Saul asked.

"Yes," Esther confirmed, "it was removed yesterday, just before replenishment."

"Is everything set?" Jacob asked.

"Yes," Ezekiel confirmed, "Saul and I both reviewed the data, just as you requested."

"Good," the elder judge said with a relieved sigh, "then we are ready to proceed." From a brown medical bag, Jacob produced two syringes. "Esther, if you would be so kind as to administer the chemical agent."

Esther took the drugs from Jacob and went, first, to Kate. "You will not be asleep, but you will feel a bit light-headed." Slipping the needle beneath Kate's skin, Esther whispered softly, "Go back home, Kate, where you belong. You take a piece of my heart with you."

Esther repeated the procedure with Matt, wishing him a safe journey in the process. "May your god be with you Matthew. And, may you and Kate find happiness back in your time."

The dome came down over each transport pod and Kate pressed her hand to the inside of the enclosure. "Goodbye, Esther. Ezekiel. Jacob and Saul."

"Goodbye Mr. and Mrs. Kelly," Jacob told them.

Ezekiel stood at the console, his hand poised above the button that would return them home. The drug they'd been given starting to take effect, Kate had to concentrate to hear Ezekiel's words. "Goodbye, Kate and Matthew. Your time here has been one we will not soon remember."

Ezekiel lowered his hand and activated the complex program.

Kate felt herself floating upward, the last sound she heard being Jacob's voice shouting, "What do you mean, not soon remembered? Ezekiel, what have you and Saul done now?"

****

The telephone on Kate's desk rang loudly, disturbing her concentration and drawing her mentally kicking and screaming from her research. "Hello?"

"Kate, sweetheart, it's me."

"Yes, Matt, what is it?"

"I was hoping I could take a rain check on lunch today."

"Rain check? Again? What is it this time?"

"We've got a stakeout going. Say you don't mind, Cricket. Please."

"I don't mind," she said simply. What good would it do to complain? Yet, deep down, she knew she should say something, anything. If not—

"Are you sure?"

"Yes, of course," she said instead, "I'm sure."

"You're a gem, Cricket, a real gem. I promise I'll make it up to you tonight."

"Matt, we need to talk."

"Yeah, Cricket, we'll talk tonight."

Damn him.

Kate stood and stretched. Half-past eleven. She'd better call and cancel their luncheon reservation. She reached for her cell and lifted it to her ear. She was about to dial when her disappointment took over.

To heck with him. She wasn't about to give up a good lunch because he wanted another crack at the bad guys. Poking her head out her office door, she called out, "Hey Sally, you want to go to Luigi's for lunch?"

"Sorry, Luigi's is a tad above my budget this week."

"My treat," Kate told her, or more precisely she thought, Matt's treat.

"Really?"

"Yes, really."

At one o'clock, she and Sally followed the hostess to the corner table. They'd no sooner taken their seats when the server was there asking for their drink order.

"I'll have a white wine," Sally told him.

Kate smiled up at the handsome young man. "Just mineral water for me."

As the waiter walked away, Sally blatantly ogled his well-muscled backside. "New talent."

Kate chuckled. "Yeah, I guess so. I don't remember seeing him before."

To Sally, her best friend and confidant, she imagined even her deepest thoughts were transparent, her feeling confirmed when Sally said, "I'm guessing you'd much rather be here with that hunk of a husband of yours. What'd he do, stand you up again?"

Kate nodded.

"You know, Kate, I—"

Whatever Sally had been about to say was lost beneath a fit of laughter.

"What?" Kate asked.

Across from her, Sally waved her arm wildly, motioning for Kate to turn around and look behind her. Shifting awkwardly in her seat, she turned in time to see Matt and their server righting themselves after an obvious collision, Kate's water and Sally's wine nothing more than a puddle at the man's feet. His angry shouts could be heard halfway across the room.

"Sorry," Kate heard Matt say, "just put it on my bill."

The man muttered something beneath his breath. Then, from out of nowhere it seemed, a tall, bearded black man came and escorted the server away.

"Matt?" She raised her head and met his sheepish grin

Matt nodded a greeting in Sally's direction.

"I think I'll just take myself off to the ladies' room," Sally announced matter-of-factly. "Come to think of it, I just remembered some work I have to do back at the office." Gathering up her purse, Sally added, "Kate, I'll catch you later."

"Thanks," Matt whispered as Sally breezed past him.

"What are you doing here?" Kate asked.

"Having lunch with my wife."

"But what about your stakeout?"

"False alarm. The perps were never there. As a matter of fact, they were arrested earlier this morning by a Detective Washington over at the tenth precinct."

"So, you decided you had time for lunch?"

"No, I decided to make time. For lunch. For you."

"Matt, we need—"

"To talk," Matt finished. "Yes, Cricket, I know. We definitely need to talk."

"But *first*, we need to *eat*." When Matt grinned broadly in her direction, she took his hand in hers and pressed it to her swollen belly. "Our baby's hungry."

A word about the author...

Like most authors, Nancy Fraser began writing at an early age, usually on the walls and with crayons or, heaven forbid, permanent markers. Her love of writing often made her the English teacher's pet, which, of course, resulted in a whole lot of teasing. Still, it was worth it.

She has published twenty-two books in both full-length and novella format. Nancy will release her 25th book in 2016. She is currently working on her next Rock and Roll novella and two new erotic romance novellas.

When not writing (which is almost never), Nancy dotes on her five wonderful grandchildren and looks forward to traveling and reading when time permits. Nancy lives in Atlantic Canada where she enjoys the relaxed pace and colorful people.

Contact Nancy at romwriter96@gmail.com

Visit Nancy at www.nancyfraser.ca